The Girls of Piazza d'Amore

A short novel

CONNIE GUZZO-MCPARLAND

.ıl.

The Girls of
Piazza d'Amore

Cover design: Debbie Geltner
Cover image: Connie Guzzo-McParland
Book design: WildElement.ca
Author photo: Magenta Photo Studio

LIBRARY AND ARCHIVES CANADA CATALOGUING IN PUBLICATION

Guzzo-McParland, Connie, 1947-, author
       The girls of Piazza d'Amore / Connie Guzzo-McParland.

Issued in print and electronic formats.
ISBN 978-1-927535-19-6 (pbk.)
ISBN 978-1-927535-20-2 (html)
ISBN 978-1-927535-22-6 (pdf)

    I. Title.

PS8613.U99G57 2013   C813'.6   C2013-902011-X
                                        C2013-902012-8

Legal Deposlt Library and Archives Canada
et Bibliothèque et Archives nationales du Québec

Linda Leith Publishing acknowledges the support of the Canada
Council for the Arts.

Printed and bound in Canada by Marquis Book Printing Inc.

Linda Leith Publishing Inc.
P.O. Box 322, Station Victoria,
Westmount, Quebec H3Z 2V8 Canada
Tel. 438-380-5485
leith.lindaleith@gmail.com
www.lindaleith.com

Dedicated to my late mother
Felicia Anania Guzzo
and all the generous women of Calabria

these are the women
who were born to give birth

they breathe only
leftover air
and speak only
when deeper voices
have fallen asleep

Gianna Patriarca
Italian Women and Other Tragedies

Prologue

As I stepped out from the lily-scented church where I had just received Communion, the soft April wind made my new organza dress flutter above my knees. It made me think of butterflies and of the feathery wings of the cherubs painted on the sky-blue church ceiling. I felt light and airy. My father clutched my free hand. His was a mason's hand, used to handling stones and gritty mortar, and it felt coarse. In my other hand, I held up my blessed palm, a large olive branch that Comare Rosaria had brought from the country the day before.

Sundays were always special in Mulirena. Palm Sunday was a child's dream. The olive branches children brought to be blessed at Mass were heavy with homemade *cullarielli,* hard doughnut-shaped cookies glazed with white sugar and tied to the branches with ribbons. My mother even managed to attach a few store-bought candies to the slender olive leaves. The branch had to be held up firmly, without tilting.

Practically all the villagers had been at this morning's Mass wearing new spring clothes. The peasant families who lived on the farms came to the village for this special occasion. The women and children sat in the pews, men circulated in the back and along the sides, girls compared new dresses, boys eyed each others' goodies, young men ogled the girls.

Men who worked in the cities were in the village for Easter. My father was home from Milan, where he worked all year long. It was the last Easter my family would spend together in Mulirena. He had come to finalize the paperwork for his visa to emigrate to Canada.

Father's thick hand kept me well anchored, as we waited for my mother and brother to make their way out of the crowded church. My family as well as my aunts, uncles, and cousins were expected for a late lunch at the home of my paternal grandparents. The day had all the prospect of a never-ending feast. And, at the end of the day, I would not feel let down, for there would still be a full week of preparations to look forward to before Easter.

Palm Sunday held the promise of Easter. In this morning's sermon, Don Raffaele had spoken about Christ's exaltation through the streets of Jerusalem. It was Christ's most joyous day, the priest had said, his

one day of celebration before the anguish of Geth-
semane, the pain of Calvary, and the glory of the
Resurrection. The priest went on and on about the
meaning of the Resurrection, but I lost interest in that
part of the story. Holy pictures of a resurrected Christ
flying to heaven in a cloudburst seemed odd to me,
and not as real as a crowd of villagers carrying Jesus
on their shoulders, cheering him on, and waving olive
branches in the air. I wanted to know more about why
things had changed so quickly for the worse for Jesus
after that day and why Judas betrayed his best friend
for only a few pennies. And I wished we would be told
more about Mary Magdalene, who truly loved Jesus
and followed him everywhere.

My mother finally made it through the throng
of parishioners bottlenecked at the narrow door. She
stopped below the steps to adjust her *pacchiana,* regional costume. First, she lowered her black velvet *mancale,*
her shawl, from her head to her back, fluffing the fes-
tive ribbons dangling from the shoulders of her vest,
and then she straightened out the *mandile –* a satiny,
rectangular head-covering, bordered with lace, held
up by pins over two braided buns on top of the head.
She lifted the floor-length pleated skirt by the hem.
This heavy wool skirt was let down at church and at
funerals, but ordinarily the women gathered it up and
then crunched and tied it into a knot at the back, creating a bustle. Underneath her skirt, she revealed two

other layers of clothes: a red flannel garment wrapped tightly around a long, white underskirt. It was a colourful but cumbersome costume that swaddled and obscured the natural contours of her young body.

Women who wore this outfit were known as *pacchiane*. Only women of my mother's generation still wore it daily, and it imposed on them a certain reserve and seriousness of demeanor — not to mention the weight of extra chores, such as gathering wood and picking olives and chestnuts, which the younger women were not expected to perform anymore. My thirty-three year old mother had been wearing it since the age of twelve — a symbol of her becoming a woman.

To go into the city, my mother borrowed clothes from one of the younger girls, changing back the minute she returned. She told me she felt naked and strange without the costume. When she sat on a doorstep, with her skirt tied at the back, sticking out like a tail, she looked like a fat hen hatching her eggs.

But coming out of church, Mother, slim and erect, looked regal. She beamed with pride as she joined us. My brother Luigi was nowhere to be seen. Mother shook her head and, with a resigned smile, said that there was no point in looking for him. He was probably home already. "He runs like a flash of lightning; you can't hold him down," she said, and Father chuckled.

We made our way down the hilly road toward

our neighbourhood, which in dialect we called *ruga*. Our next-door neighbour, Comare Rosaria, and her daughter, Lucia, joined us.

Father struck up a conversation with Amadeo, the village band director, who stopped walking whenever he wanted to emphasize a point. He complained that the young guys didn't want to know anything about *solfeggio* or the study of arias. "They only want to play tangos on their cheap, out-of-tune accordions," he said, doing a little dance number and playing an imaginary accordion. Then he raised his hands in exasperation as we approached our *ruga*. A gramophone was blasting from the house of *U Grancu*.

Totu, a young man who courted Lucia, waved at me from *U Grancu*'s window. Totu never resisted pinching my cheeks whenever he had a chance. His uncle, Don Cesare, who owned a small truck, a *furgoncino*, and often drove to Catanzaro, had bought him some new records. The season's favourite pop singer, Georgio Consolini, whined the popular *Terra Straniera* – a sweetly melodic, plaintive song that melted our hearts.

"With a voice like that…," Amadeo said. "But he is wasting it on these *canzonette*. *Mah!*"

Then the song screeched to a stop and was replaced by another, sung in a woman's chirpy voice. The sound filled the neighbourhood. It was an infectious song, and it prompted the young girls to open

5

their windows to the new sun, to new loves, and to their dreams. I had heard the song a couple of times already and knew all the words:

> *Aprite le finestre al nuovo sole,*
> *È primavera, é primavera*
>
> *Lasciate entrare un poco d'aria pura*
> *Con il profumo dei giardini e prati in fior*
>
> *Aprite le finestre ai nuovi sogni,*
> *Bambine belle innamorate*
>
> *È forse il più bel sogno che sognate*
> *Sarà domani la felicità.*

Part I

I was nine years old on that Palm Sunday in 1955, and I was certain that happiness was within reach of a window opened to the scent of gardens and orchards in bloom.

The tomorrow anticipated by the song has come and gone many times since then. Yet another spring has ended. In fact, it's close to summer in Montreal – the long weekend in May when gardeners in northern climates can plant their begonias without fear of frost. I'm sitting on my balcony with a coffee and a pile of yellowed composition notebooks, as contented as a lizard basking in the first warm day of the season. I don't have a garden to plant, but I do have the weekend all to myself, and I've promised myself to do nothing more than read and write. It's a well-deserved break. Yesterday evening, I succeeded in exchanging the winter clothes in my closet for summer wear stored in the basement locker, a banal ritual performed at the start of every new season that nonetheless gives me the illusion of restoring order in my life. This time I had another, more ambitious mission that had been on my mind for months. Buried at the very back of the locker, under boxes of used clothing and discarded furniture, was the rusty green metal trunk that had travelled with my family when we immigrated to Canada. I remembered its contents well – obsolete remnants of the old life that had been last aired out when my mother and I moved into this apartment years ago: a black velvet shawl and a lacy *mandile* that she bought over as a souvenir of her regional costume; embroidered sheets, pillowcases, and a damask bedspread that have never been used since they don't fit a Canadian standard double bed; yellowed letters and photographs; and various other trinkets that will never be used or displayed in my apartment. My mother no longer lives with me, but the old trunk has stayed in the locker. Discarding it would seem sacrilegious.

What I sought out last evening was on the very top of the memorabilia – some Italian books and the composition notebooks I had kept from my elementary school days in Mulirena. The notebooks are filled with notes and anecdotes of village life. I was especially interested in an unfinished manuscript – my very first attempt at writing. Over the years, I had often thought of the unwritten stories buried in the trunk, but never long enough to want to rummage around in the cluttered locker. I have rekindled my old passion for writing stories and have registered in a writing class. With the long weekend ahead of me, I finally hauled out the old trunk.

This morning, with the warm sun drawing me outdoors, I spread all this material out on the patio table. A blank postcard of the Rock of Gibraltar sticks out of the familiar copy of a thick novel, *I Promessi Sposi*, by Alessandro Manzoni, a book I received as a gift on my last day in Mulirena. A Roman steward had given me the card as a souvenir of the trip. With the novel are a prayer book with a mother-of-pearl cover, a manual on masonry that my father had brought from Milan, and a book on the history of Mulirena which was sent to us a few years after we left. The cover shows a photograph of the village.

Mulirena was built on a hill, so we were forever walking up and down. Approaching it from nearby Amato, the village looked like a pyramid of whitewashed houses with red roofs, with the bell-tower of one church forming its peak and another church squatting at the lower edge. A visiting bishop once compared the village, in his sermon, to a large family living in a multilevel house with many rooms, held together by the two churches. What the bishop may not have realized was that the two churches were called not by their proper names, but by *a ghiesa e supra,* the church at the top, and *a ghiesa e sutta,* the church at the bottom, and that they kept the villagers apart rather than uniting them. The main parish church, Santa Lucia, the one on the hill, was frequented by the Christian Democrats, the well-to-do, and friends of the only priest in the village. The other church, Madonna del Rosario, was favoured by those who opposed the Democrats and the priest. At election time, functions held at either church were boycotted by half the village.

What brought early inhabitants to settle in this part of the Appenines, which is not particularly fertile, seems to have been the fine sand from its rocky soil. Legend has it that the village's original name, Migliarina, is derived from *megghia rina*, best sand. This early name might have changed to Mulirena over the years in reference to the mules or *muli e rina* used to cart the sand from the riverbed and up the mountain roads to the village proper. The sand also provided the raw material for making stone. The men of the village developed a reputation as fine stonemasons, *muratori* – builders of walls.

Amato was no further away than the length of a soccer field, but the villages faced each other across a deep ravine. The road that led to Mulirena from Amato – and from the rest of the world – was the shape of a horseshoe. It ran along the ravine on the Amato side for about a kilometre, turned sharply across a bridge, and then sharply again toward Mulirena.

A kilometre off the road on the Amato side, just before the bridge, stood the Timpa, a low, wide mountain that had been quarried for as long as anyone could remember. This was the furthest we could walk before feeling we were entering Amato territory. The residents of Amato considered us *cafoni,* uncouth mountain peasants, while the Mulerinesi snickered at the Amatesi for being pretentious snobs while dying of hunger, *muarti e hhame.* The two villages were like Siamese twins joined together at the neck but wanting badly to keep their distance from each other. If one village sneezed, the other, jolted by the vibrations, would sneeze back harder.

We girls never ventured as far as the Timpa alone. It was a place for boys to meet at night, to sneak a smoke, and find privacy. During the day at the Timpa, there was always a cloud of dust swirling around the beaten-up trucks that regularly drove in from Amato, loaded the dusty crop of rocks and gravel, and then drove off to Marcellinara and its freight trains. No one ever asked what the stones were used for. Every afternoon, sirens went off to warn people to go indoors. That's when the mountain was dynamited and rocks burst up like fireworks into the sky. It was only logical to use the Timpa for real fireworks on the feast of Santa Lucia. Then, everyone gathered across the ravine to watch and applaud as the mountain exploded with lights.

The bridge at the bend of the horseshoe was built high over a cleared section of the ravine. Immediately after the bridge, the road turned toward Mulirena, and, from it, one could see the top of a long, stone staircase that gradually descended into the gorge. At its base lay the Funtanella, the village's communal fountains and everyone's favourite meeting place. My grandfather liked to claim that this structure had been built by the Romans, but the village was in fact founded in the sixteenth century. And why would the Romans have bothered to build anything so deep into the mountains? At the centre of the structure was a long, carved wall. Water flowed from the mouths of its gargoyles and chubby-cheeked faces and into a shallow, waist-high basin. The water jugs were placed in the basin to be filled with spring water, which was renowned for its clarity and coolness, and which was preferred to the water from the aqueduct. From the two sides of the fountain wall ran a system of long furrows, all along the sides of the ravine, into which the water overflowed. Some of the water fell into low troughs for watering animals. Most of it was channeled into a more recent addition: a large, cement basin separated into four smaller ones that were used by the women for washing clothes.

This was the village's gift to the women. Before the basin, the women had had to carry the *lessiva,* the heavy straw baskets in which the dirty clothes had steeped in a mixture of water and ashes from the fireplaces, to the river, la Fiumara, which was a long way from the village. Now the weekly wash at la Funtanella had become a social event for the women, who chatted, laughed, and sometimes sang as they washed. The little girls went along and, propped up on a rock, were given small items to wash.

Coincidentally, or so it might seem, groups of men – especially single men – took their *passeggiata* at the same time as the women did their laundry or filled their jugs with drinking water. But everyone understood that the Funtanella was the place to see and to be seen by the opposite sex. The men would walk, arm in arm, sometimes speaking in whispers to one another as though talking about forbidden matters, and sometimes arguing loudly about politics. They always stopped on the bridge. The women would be scrubbing away on the concrete washboards below, trying to get the dirty laundry as white as possible – their husband's shirts, the baby's diapers, the long strips of white cotton used for swaddling babies like mummies, the heavy bed sheets, their own long white shirts, and those mysterious diaper-like squares of white cloth that they hid at the bottom of their baskets. No matter how hard they beat those *pezze,* or rubbed them over the hard slabs until their knuckles turned red and cracked from the cold water and the caustic homemade soap, the women could never get rid of the shadows of the stubborn, brownish-red stains.

From the bridge, the men smoked, joked, argued

and pretended indifference to what was going on below, but, depending on who was there, their gazes would dart down to the watery women's domain, down the winding steps to a floor made of ancient stones that were round and smooth from years of wear, and that were also mossy, wet, and very slippery.

The line of homes along the road and the periphery of the village started at the bridge. Their long balconies overlooked the Timpa, the cypresses of the cemetery in Amato, and the ravine. The village's garbage and bedpans had been dumped into the ravine for ages; but, all one saw, looking over the edge, were the thick bushes and the trees growing at a slant over the precipice. Along the whole length of the ravine, a stone parapet, as high as a child's shoulders, provided some protection for the children and a favourite place for men to sit and cool off on hot summer nights. It was also a great spot to wait for people to come in and out of Amato.

The road continued into the main street, Via Roma, which went down toward the poorer part of the village in one direction, and, in the other, up a series of cobblestone steps to the upper church.

The main piazza, at Piano Valle, sprawled just below the cobblestone steps and was the dividing line between the upper and lower parts of the village. In this area stood the school, the town hall, and many shops. Peppino's bar was the centre of attraction for the men. They sat on the chairs outside, sipping coffee and talking politics all day long. During the heated election periods, from a balcony above the school, the Christian Democrats and their adversaries shouted their *comizi,* which incited applause, catcalls, and the occasional fistfights. In quieter times, during the major religious feasts, people brought chairs from home and sat around the piazza to watch the movies that Don Raffaele projected on a large open-air screen.

Via Roma ran like a herringbone all down the spine of the village, with narrow alleys projecting off either side and then breaking up into other smaller alleys. Here and there, along this main street, were little squares, not quite piazzas, of which there was only one, but little enclaves of houses built around flat common areas and drinking fountains. The people who drank from the same fountain were identified by these *rughe*. They helped each other during harvests, and in times of crisis, but also fought and argued with each other – much like brothers and sisters. On summer evenings, the women congregated around one of the doorsteps, reciting the rosary, gossiping and telling stories, while the kids counted stars and chased fireflies.

We called the *ruga* in which I lived Piazza Don Carlo, though the more archaic Piano Don Carlo was engraved on a stone tablet on the corner wall of Don Cesare's home. There were five families living in this square, opening up onto the main road and an alley.

Our next door neighbours were Rosaria Abiusi and her family on one side, and Don Cesare, the wealthiest man in the village, on the other. Directly across from our house lived Nicola, known as *U Grancu*, the Crab, and his younger sister, Tina. The rest of his family had immigrated to Canada, but he had been refused a visa because of his disabilities. Besides being very short, almost a dwarf, he had a crooked spine, one hip higher than the other, and walked with a limp, moving his arms. Tina was engaged to be married, and had chosen to remain in Mulirena. *U Grancu* never set foot outside his home, but he knew everyone's business. He spent most of the money his parents sent him from Canada on books, magazines, and gramophone records. His house was a meeting place for all the unemployed young men.

Next to *U Grancu*, and diagonally across from my house, lived Anna, *a pazza* – the crazy one. Her house had seen better days. It had been bombed during the war and had never been repaired. The old woman and her husband made do with one room that was no better than a stable. She had not always been crazy – only since the war. Her son was one of a handful of men who had never returned. It was assumed he had been taken prisoner in Germany, but his death was never confirmed. The villagers were not too surprised by Anna's deterioration.

As we reached Piazza Don Carlo, Father and I joined Mother, Comare Rosaria, Lucia and Tina, who were standing around the fountain. The water from the aqueduct was cut off in the middle of the day. As the days got hotter, the water supply was shut off earlier and earlier, and the fountain became a seating area.

An itinerant photographer walked slowly up from the alley with his heavy equipment on his shoulder. My mother suggested that the family have a photograph taken, now that we were all dressed up. It would be the last photo taken of us before Father's departure. In anticipation of her own emigration, Mother would soon be trading in her costume for regular clothes. My brother Luigi, true to his impulsive nature, and much to Mother's annoyance, had already changed into his summer shorts. Father was in his new brown suit, which would accompany him to the new country. My new organza dress was baby blue with crisp flounces on the bodice and hem.

The photographer carefully aligned his camera on a wooden tripod. He placed Father and Mother side by side, Luigi on Mother's right, with her hand gently resting on his shoulder, and me on Father's left, his arm hugging me firmly. Rosaria's two sons, Alfonso and Giacomo walked by and stopped to watch the photographer. After the picture had been taken, the two young women, Tina and Lucia, who had been joined by their friend Aurora, teased Father about his new suit and his impending trip.

"They have coffee cups as big as *pisciaturi*," Tina said. "They drink it by the litre because they work day and night."

"If you have work, food, and a bed, what else do you want?" Comare Rosaria added.

Lucia turned to Mother, "Terè, they say that Canadian women go crazy for Italian men."

"That's the last thing that Comare Teresa is worried about," Rosaria replied, and everyone laughed.

Professore Nucci, a friend of Father's, who had joined the discussion, started an argument. He wasn't really a professor; he just liked to be called *Professore*. Someone heard him introducing himself to an outsider as Professore Nucci, and the title had stuck. He was a bachelor at thirty and lived with his two spinster sisters, who looked after him. He received a small stipend from the village for doing minor secretarial work, but he spent most of the day walking up and down the main street in a pensive mood, his arms behind his back, a baton in one hand. Sometimes he would stop, look up into the air, and move his head as though he were reviewing a musical score. He played the clarinet and was the assistant to the village bandleader. He liked to think of himself as a maestro; sometimes people humoured him with that title. He had no relatives overseas to sponsor him and therefore no chance of emigrating.

"I wouldn't go to Canada if they paid me in gold," he said.

"Don't worry, *professò*. They only pay for professors like you in Mulirena. Everywhere else you have to work," said Alfonso, who had a bone to pick with the town hall for having refused him a position. Everyone laughed. The professor pretended not to hear them and cornered Father, who was holding me by the hand.

"Peppé, let's be serious. Are you really going? What do you think you're going to find there?"

"I'm going there to work, like everyone else."

"Do you know they build their houses out of wood?" he asked.

"*Professò*, you don't have a family, so you don't know how it is. For me it's an opportunity."

"*Mah!* Are you joking? What opportunity? You are a *mastro*. You have worked in stone all your life, you have built palaces in Milan out of granite and marble, and now you are going to build barns. You're a smart man and a musician. Let these *cafoni* go there."

"If they give me work, I'll build my house out of cement and marble," answered Father. I was surprised at how enthusiastic he sounded with his friend. At home, the evening before, he'd said that, when he received the official papers in Milan, he'd been almost sorry he had initiated the immigration procedures. "I didn't jump up and down like the others, as if I had won the lottery," he had said.

21

The professor made a last, grand gesture with his arms, addressing everyone now. "I'd rather eat bread and onions all my life and enjoy this sun. Where else are you going to find a day like today? *Pane, amore e fantasia,*" he said with a flourish of his baton, repeating the title of a popular film we had all watched with glee a few months earlier. The allusion seemed to fit what he was trying to say, though his meaning was not completely clear. He resumed his perpetual walk in the too-tight, too-short beige cotton suit he had been wearing for years.

Some of the children were playing *girotondo*. Mother took my branch and told me to go ahead and join them.

Maybe it was the song about spring and sunshine that had filled the air, but, one by one, all the kids and the adults from the *ruga,* as well as others who happened to be walking by, joined the circle. The circle got so large it covered the whole square. It went around and around, past Comare Rosaria's house, past *U Grancu*'s, where Totu waved at us. The singing got louder and louder. I kept looking at the adults' faces. I couldn't believe that everyone – including my mother, my father, Comare Rosaria, Lucia, Tina, and Aurora – were playing like children and singing our song.

We ran around in a circle singing, "*Giro giro tondo, com'é bello il mondo.*" At the end of each refrain, "*Casca la terra, tutti giu' per terra,*" we let ourselves drop to the

22

ground, laughing. Then we got up and started again, the circle turning faster and faster.

But then, someone pointed in the direction of old Anna's house.

"Watch out, *a pazza, a pazza, u pisciaturu.*"

Old Anna came out of her door, carrying a big chamber pot, yelling at us to stop making noise. She hurled the contents of the pot at the crowd, and everyone scattered in different directions. "Come back! It's only water," I cried. I expected the singing would resume. No one came back.

I watched Mother go inside our house. Father disappeared into the alley, motioning downward with his arms. "Don't bother me with this anymore. It's children's stuff. Leave me alone." I was angry, angry at the old woman and at her son in Germany for ruining my feast, especially angry at Father for dismissing me so callously. I closed my eyes, and began to spin round and round, until I fell, exhausted and dizzy, alone in the middle of the square.

After that Easter, as Father prepared to leave for Canada, things seemed to be changing in Mulirena. I remembered sensing the transformations overtaking the village, though I could not explain them at the time. A curious feeling hung over the village – a vague sensation that Mulirena itself, along with the people around me, was changing into something different from what I had known. Suddenly I took notice of people and events as if seeing them for the first time and from a distance, aware that soon I would be leaving them. The changes excited me, but they also left me sad and a little apprehensive. It was like being given new toys with which to play, in exchange for old beloved ones.

My mother often spoke of how the village had teemed with people and activity before the war, and before mass emigration. When I lived there, the village had a population of about fifteen hundred. "Four houses and four cats" – that is how we spoke about it after we left.

Like many mountain villages in Calabria, Mulirena was built around a steep, winding road that came to a dead end. A first-time visitor could only wonder why anyone would settle there. One either became resigned to living the simple life of the village or looked for a future elsewhere.

"Here, there is no *avvenire*," I remember the villagers saying. They meant that nothing new or exciting would ever come our way.

"We must leave for the sake of the children," was another pronouncement, which became the mantra for the exodus, not that we children ever complained, for we were the least deprived.

I was born as the war ended, but I felt as if I had lived through it all. My mother spoke about it continually, especially comparing the present conditions of the village with those of the war years when the Fascist government rationed bread, flour, oil, and sugar at subsistence level, and raw hunger was the order of the day. So were lice infestations and ringworm, in spite of *Il Duce's* call to greatness. With all the able-bodied men away in the army, the women were left to fend for themselves, taking care of farms, animals, the old, and the young. Worried about the lack of news from husbands, sons, and brothers fighting in unknown places and for unknown reasons, they were also kept awake at night by sirens and occasional bombings. Yet, Mother claimed, they were still better off than those living in the northern cities. Many refugees from those shelled-out places sought refuge in the desolate villages and avoided starvation by sharing wild field greens, rough yellow cornbread, and gritty polenta with the villagers.

"In the *paese* you never *really* starve," people said. This had been their only consolation.

A decade after the fall of Fascism, life in the village should have resumed its placid pre-war pattern. But the strong odour of DDT mixed with the stench of urine-soaked diapers in the damp, whitewashed bedrooms of stone houses must have been nauseating and stifling for the returning soldiers who saw no reward in sight for their years of combat against and for the Germans. My grandfather never stopped talking about how the Italian army had been betrayed, by whom, he never said. Mussolini's failures and defeat must have dealt a heavy blow, not only to the regional economy, but to the psyches of his men who had been pumped up with dreams of returning to the glory days of a mythical Roman empire. They replaced the Roman salute with another well-known Italian gesture – that of slapping the right arm while bending it at the elbow – also directed towards Rome. I guess that too much had been shaken up in Mulirena for life to resume serenely.

On their return, the restless men had found jobs rebuilding the war ruins of Cassino, Naples, and Rome. Then they gravitated toward Milan, where wages were paid more regularly than in the southern cities. The Mulirena men still complained that the cost of city living made it impossible for them to settle their families there. So, for years, the men came and went, while the women and children remained alone and rarely travelled beyond the nearby village.

This pattern began to change when the gateways to the Americas opened up, and men bought one-way tickets out of the village. We were used to seeing the men leave for the cities of the north without much commotion, since they returned every chance they got. But when women and children packed their trunks into Don Cesare's *furgoncino*, the only vehicle in the village, the departures were accompanied by tears and screams. We children followed the truck as far as we could run until it disappeared in clouds of dust beyond the Timpa.

After Easter, my whole family travelled to Rome for father's visa, and before that, Don Cesare drove us to Catanzaro, the provincial city, a number of times to get outfitted with new shoes and clothes for the trip to Rome. The sights, smells, and noises of the two cities were a jolting reminder of the changes that awaited me when I, too, would leave the sleepy village for a completely unknown place across the ocean.

When I returned from Rome wearing new clothes, I felt all grown up. I spent less and less time with my school friends and more at the seamstress's shop with the older girls, Lucia, Tina and Aurora. The trio of girls was inseparable and I was their mascot. I followed them in their evening *passeggiate,* became their accomplice in their hidden amorous adventures, and listened to the secrets that girls in Mulirena only revealed to each other and never, but never, to their mothers.

The most remarkable change for me that summer was that, whatever stories I heard at the seamstress's shop or saw happening around me, I replayed in my mind, like memorizing lines of a poem. I imagined those stories as playing out on the big screen that Don Raffaele set up outdoors on special occasions. I never saw myself as a participant, at the time, as much as a narrator, and Mulirena became the setting for my own versions of *Pane, amore e fantasia* with Gina Lollobrigida, or – my very favourite film – *Le Ragazze di Piazza di Spagna,* about three seamstresses of a couture house in Rome who ride a *Vespa* and gather on the steps of the famous Piazza to eat lunch and talk of their love lives. I daydreamed about riding a Vespa with my friends and sitting on those steps in the sunset.

Lucia and Aurora were considered two of the prettiest girls in the village, Aurora with long, almost blonde hair and grey eyes, and Lucia with curly, dark hair that framed her face like a soft cushion of puffy springs. They were both slim, but Lucia was more petite and vivacious. Lucia was very proud of her hair, parting it in the centre with a wet comb before going out, conscious that it was part of her reputation as a village belle, together with her heart-shaped mouth and spirited black eyes, and a beauty mark like an exclamation point below her lip. Tina was a brown-haired, plainer girl, but tall for a girl of the village. She was always cheerful and liked telling jokes. Everyone admired her long legs and big bust.

We girls all lived in the same square, Lucia and I even in the same house. The L-shaped row of houses that faced the road and Piazza Don Carlo had once been one large mansion which had housed Don Cesare Cicala's family. Over the years, it was subdivided between Don Cesare, my mother's family and Rosaria's family, the Abiusi.

Aurora's parents – Domenico, known as Micu, and Paola – were peasants who worked for Don Cesare and often spent the night at the *casale* on the farm. Aurora never worked on the farm, but attended school in the village. As a child, she often slept at Don Cesare's house to keep his wife company when he was away. As she got older, she did little chores around the house, but she was never considered a maid.

The backs of the houses formed an enclosed courtyard with an orchard, which was accessible only to Don Cesare. His home still had all the semblance of a mansion, with a protective stone wall around its entrance, a front courtyard, and large rooms with high ceilings. It was the grandest home, not only of the square, but of the village, and it gave all who lived in Piazza Don Carlo a sense of importance.

Lucia, Tina, and Aurora had grown up together, and Lucia and Aurora had been desk friends throughout school. School desks were built for two, and friends were usually allowed to share the same desk; they called one other *cumpagne e bancu*. Desk friends developed a very close relationship. They shared the same inkwell, borrowed one another's pencils and erasers, learned to read each other's handwriting, and found ways to cheat and copy from one another. If during the course of the year the friendship ended, however, having to sit so close became torture.

The three older girls' education had stopped after

the fifth grade. They would have had to travel to the provincial city of Catanzaro to continue, but none of their parents could afford the expense. A girl's only possible occupation was to work for free for the local dressmaker in exchange for learning the trade. Giovanna, the seamstress, took me in as an apprentice that summer in spite of my young age, because she and my mother were good friends. I was very mature for my age, everyone told me. I was given the task of basting seams before the pieces of cloth were sewn together into skirts, dresses, and blouses. Neither Tina nor Lucia was particularly adept at sewing. They spent time chatting and laughing at the shop, but their sewing skills never progressed beyond basting seams like me. Aurora applied herself more, making and cutting patterns, and doing finer needlework. I often saw her sitting on Donna Rachele's balcony, mending clothes.

Aurora was as well-groomed as any of the other village girls. Her fair skin and hair and large, light-grey eyes set her apart, but her fragile beauty was somehow tarnished by the fact that her mother was a peasant, a *Ciociara*, originally from somewhere near Cassino. The gossip in the village was that Paola slept with the *padrone,* and that the reason he was so kind to Aurora was that he felt a fatherly love toward her.

Aurora had a very friendly disposition and went in and out of people's houses with more ease than was usually considered acceptable, but this was easily explained by the fact that her mother was an outsider. Aurora spent a lot of time with the Abiusi's, even eating her meals there whenever she played with Lucia. Comare Rosaria called Aurora *a zingarella* or the little gypsy.

In the summer evenings, the three girls would go out with their water jugs for a *passeggiata* to the Funtanella. I followed them. I was a useful little helper, since I distributed all their love notes back and forth. Each of the three girls had a boyfriend courting her. By the time they were fifteen or sixteen, it had become common knowledge that Lucia "made love" with Don Cesare's nephew, Totu; Tina with Michele, a young tailor who looked like the actor Rossano Brazzi; and Aurora with Saverio, a blacksmith who was a close friend of Michele.

Fare l'amore was what the ritual of courtship was called. Many marriages, though arranged by families, in reality entailed personal selections. In the restrictive society of the village, where women and men knew to keep their distance, sexual interest started young. Most teenaged girls strolling to the Funtanella were conscious of the long glances young men gave them. If interest was kindled, a young man would station himself under the girl's window, and, if she were keen, she would peek out. A few words might be exchanged, but lovers mostly communicated with their eyes. Whenever a young man slouched against a wall and looked up at a balcony, people would say that the couple *faceva l'amore,* was making love. Some couples "made love" this way for years, every day for hours, before they were ready for the official engagement. If the families were agreeable to the relationship, they would pretend not to notice the young man gawking at their window. When the girl spent too much time on her balcony, her parents might threaten to shower the man with dirty dishwater, or worse. When the family objected, the wooing would be kept discreet.

In the three corners of Piazza Don Carlo, there were three girls making love, often at the same time, with the three young men stationed beneath Lucia's, Tina's and Don Cesare's balconies, while I sat on my balcony, like a little guard watching their every gesture.

One afternoon, on his habitual walk, Professore Nucci stopped by our square and stood for a few minutes staring, taking in the scene of the three couples making love. Maybe emboldened by each other's presence and the absence of adults in their households on that particular day, the girls leaned over the balcony rails and went beyond the permissible silent eye contact, giggling and responding to the words of love whispered by the men below, who gestured with outstretched arms as if wanting to touch them. Aurora's mother had left a basket of freshly-picked figs on the fountain wall for all to taste. The men gorged themselves on the first ripe figs of the season, savoring the juicy red pulp while looking up at the girls with yearning eyes.

"*Che bellezza! Piazza Don Carlo é una vera piazza d'amore,*" exclaimed the Professore, startling the three couples from the spell of unrestrained passion they dared to display out in the open for all to see. He declared Piazza Don Carlo a piazza of love.

"*Bravo, maestro,*" Totu shot back clapping. Everyone laughed and applauded while the Professore bowed, picked a fig from the basket, and walked down the hill.

After the girls recounted the incident at the seamstress's shop, Giovanna took to calling them "*l'amuruse,*" the girls in love, and whenever she chided them for talking too much, or not paying attention to their work, she'd say, "Where do you think you are, at the *Piazza d'Amore?*"

When the three girls walked to the Funtanella for water and passed by their boyfriends, on the bridge, before descending the steps to the fountain, one of the boys would hand me a candy with a little note around it, which I passed on to the girl it was addressed to.

I knew to keep the letters secret, especially from Lucia's brother, who was known to have a bad temper and to dislike Totu. One evening, when he caught the two whispering together in the alley next to the house, Alfonso dragged Lucia by her long hair and kicked her inside, yelling as he shut the door, "Stay inside and don't let me find you going around like a *zingara* again." This didn't keep Lucia from going to the Funtanella the next evening and giving me a note to pass on to Totu.

Alfonso always seemed angry at someone. I never saw him smiling. Totu was an innocent bystander. He and Alfonso had never had any fights, but Alfonso had an ongoing feud with Don Cesare, his second cousin, and the reason he disliked Totu was that Totu was Don Cesare's favourite nephew.

"I don't understand why your brother is so against him," Giovanna told Lucia after the hair-pulling incident. "Totu is the best catch for any girl. He's good-looking, smart, and has a future ahead of him. Does your brother think you're going to find better than that?"

"I don't care what my brother thinks," Lucia answered, not very concerned. "He's just jealous. I love Totu, and he loves me. That's all that counts."

I lived for those evening *passeggiate* and never wanted to miss one, often arguing with my mother over what to wear. After a light dinner of tomato salad with a piece of *provolone* cheese or *mortadella*, she washed my face, combed my hair away from my face, and tied the top with a large pink bow before letting me run out to join the trio.

Thinking back to those summers, I realize how easily we girls let life take its course and shrugged off as normal the contradictions present in small parochial villages: love and hatred, friendship and rivalry, generosity of spirit and petty jealousy. My world then just *was*. It was going to *la Funtanella* with Lucia and other older girls every evening to fetch water in the two-handled clay jugs that we carried, not on our heads like the older women, but balanced on a hip, which forced us to walk with a slanted and languid gait. At times, the spring water gushed in tiny torrents out of the mouths of the stone gargoyles; at other times it just trickled down. And sometimes, in the arid spells of summer, the mouths were dry, gaping holes, making the gargoyles look like the catechism book pictures of the desperate, damned souls destined to be thirsty forever. But the flow of the Funtanella was never questioned then. For many years after settling in Montreal, I'd replay those past moments in my mind, like a bedtime story that children read over and over, each time finding new pleasures or new questions to ask. Though these memories have become less frequent over time, they come accompanied by small pangs of discomfort, a tightening of the chest. I remember reading that, for some, having had a happy childhood is almost as painful as having suffered an unhappy one. It feels like a persistent ache of yearning, like the grief for a lost love.

The summer slid past us, and then Father left. He left the village so often that the actual parting didn't leave a vivid memory. We all knew the absence would be short; he would call for the family as soon as he could.

My father was portly and solidly built. He had a large forehead with a receding hairline, prominent red cheeks, and a dimple on his chin. He looked like a jolly ice-cream vendor who would give second scoops for free. He was one of the few men in Mulirena who had no enemies; he was known as a friend who could never refuse anyone a favour. Everyone liked him, especially the children. When he returned from Milan, he always came back with small toys for all. When the children of the *ruga* passed him at the bar, he bought them candies or ice cream.

The summer of 1955 was the longest period that Father spent with the family, and I discovered things about him that I had never noticed before. He liked reading as much as I did, and, for someone with only a fifth-grade education, he could discuss politics and music as well as the other more educated men of the village. He liked to peruse a thick book on ornamental architecture, with pictures of different styles of stone columns, cornices, and friezes, that he had studied from in Milan. He said he wanted to be well prepared for working in the new country.

After his return from the war, Father had tried his luck working in Monte Cassino with his father. There was lots of construction going in at that bombed city, but earnings were meager and often not paid on time – or not at all. Like many other stonemasons from the village, he eventually found regular work in Milan.

His seventeen-year-old brother, Vincenzo, was anxious to earn his own money, and Father brought him there as his assistant.

On a routine climb up a scaffold, Vincenzo fell and, right under Father's eyes, died instantly from a blow to the head. This happened when I was a baby, but later I heard stories of Father's return to the village late at night to give his mother the news. He had promised his mother he'd take care of her youngest child in Milan. Unable to face her, he had his best friend prepare the family before Father showed up to ask for his mother's forgiveness. He had to bury his brother in Milan since the cost of transporting the body was prohibitive. The death left a wound in the heart of my father's family that would never heal. I always remembered my Nanna Caterina dressed in black, with a sad, drawn-out look on her face.

Father was the only remaining son of his family, but he had four sisters. Two, married with children, still lived in the village, one had joined her husband in Argentina, and the eldest had settled in Montreal. It was this sister, my aunt Rosina, who sponsored Father and made it possible for him to emigrate.

My Nanna and all of my aunts had broad faces with strong jaw lines, wide hips, and solid legs. I was often told I had taken after that side of the family because of my large face and high forehead, but my mother worried because I was too skinny for her liking.

She used to make me drink *Ferrochina*, an iron-based drink, beaten into a raw egg every morning.

My mother's side of the family was better off than my father's. They owned land, a grocery store run by her brother Pietro, and a bakery adjacent to the store. My mother worked at the bakery a few days a week, helping her widowed mother bake round firm breads almost as big as a bicycle wheel. I loved going to the bakery for lunch when my mother had a slice of warm freshly baked bread ready for me with a chunk of *provolone* cheese from the store.

In the evenings, Father took it upon himself to give reading lessons to an illiterate young peasant who lived in an alley near our house. By the end of the summer, the eighteen-year-old could write his name and read from my second-grade reader.

My mother's two cousins, who worked in Rome as tailors, were also in the village for the summer, and in the evenings we would all gather at their place. The men played *briscola,* and the women played *scopa* with the children. After the card games, Father took to reading from a book about the true-life story of the bandit Giuliano, who hid in the mountains with a woman until he was betrayed by one of his men and gunned down by a lawman. Father assigned roles from the story to himself and my cousins. He played Giuliano, whom everyone admired for his daring and generosity toward the poor peasants who helped him dodge the law.

During the day, Father spent most of his free time walking with his friends and discussing politics, though he was not as passionate about the topic as some of the others. He was in a very delicate position. My mother's family had always been Christian Democrats, while his father opposed the party.

The only time I remember my parents arguing was when Mother found out that Father had lent money to his best friend. Father insisted that friendship was more valuable than money. Mother agreed about the friendship, but this friend was not trustworthy. He never worked, was rumoured to cheat on his wife, and had taken advantage of Father's generosity before.

"What upsets me is that you believe everything your friends tell you," she argued.

"And you worry about a few lire when I'll soon be working in America," he replied. "America" was any country on the far side of the ocean.

"I don't like counting my money until I have it in my hands."

Father kicked a chair against a wall. "You women are always right," he said, and he went out to meet his friends at the bar. Unlike my short strong-boned aunts, my mother was tall and thin, with a delicate face, but her frail appearance was deceptive. When she put her foot down to me and my brother, and sometimes even to my father, no pleading could change her mind.

Before that outbreak, I had never known my father to get easily upset, but a few days later, he was livid when a clerk at the post office told him he was too busy to serve him. Father lodged a written complaint against the clerk. Then later he started a petition to have my third-grade teacher removed from Mulirena for incompetence. I had told him repeatedly that we used to spend the day in her class chasing flies. Both times, Mother told him that he was wasting his time, but Father said he did it out of principle, that people in Milan would never put up with the inefficiency of public workers as they did in Calabria.

"Why can't we make any progress here, like in the North?" he said.

"Your father doesn't really want to leave," Mother told us after one of his outbursts. "He'd be happier if we all moved to Milan."

When Father left in September, Mother kept telling everyone that, for her, the main advantage of Father going to Canada was that the family would be able to live together in one place.

Before leaving, without telling my mother, he bought my brother a bicycle.

To me he made a promise. One day, in the piazza, he sat me in Don Cesare's car and said, "When you turn twenty-one in America, I'll get you a car. You'll learn how to drive like one of the *americane* in the movies. You can be whatever you want to be there…

40

a teacher… a lawyer… a doctor."

"I want to be a teacher," I said.

When I was not in school or at the seamstress's shop, I spent my free time in church. Every time I went to confession, Don Raffaele would urge me, "Pray that you become a saint." Maybe Don Raffaele said this to everyone he confessed, but he singled me out enough times to make me feel he was grooming me for sainthood. Even before I could read, I belonged to the Catholic Action Movement. One could belong to this group from childhood to adulthood; each age group was identified by a different name, from the *Piccolissime* to *Donne*. Boys and girls met separately once a week with a group leader who read stories about saintly people who dedicated their lives to the service of others. Every month we received a magazine from Rome that taught us about the Catholic missions in Africa, South America, and many other parts of the world. There were rules and regulations, and each year we were given different *parole d'ordine,* words to live by. The one I remember best was *saper sorridere sempre* – know how to smile always. The selfless saintly life was what we were taught to aim for, so each night I prayed, "God, help me become a saint."

I didn't imagine myself as just any old saint, one who simply prayed, went around blessing people, and performing miracles, but rather the type who earned her halo through acts of charity and heroism. We children used to exchange holy pictures of saints who were our heroes. Saint Maria Goretti was one of my favourites. She was a young girl who let herself be beaten to death rather than succumb to a rapist. Naturally, she was the patron saint of chastity. One picture of her was worth two or three ordinary ones. It was the same for Saint John Bosco, who was everyone's favourite. The patron saint of children, he helped wayward kids find their way. In pictures, he is depicted with children staring at him adoringly, like a teen idol.

While I was still in kindergarten, and still a *Piccolissima,* Don Raffaele chose me to recite a poem in church on the occasion of the Pope's birthday. Mother read it out loud until I learned it perfectly. At the altar, standing on a chair in front of the microphone, I saw the sea of faces looking up at me, and I panicked. My mind went blank. The priest came up next to me, and whispered the first line, "*Noi siam le piccolissime del nostro buon Gesù.*" I recited the rest. Afterwards I ran to my mother and hid my face in her lap, ashamed that I had forgotten my lines. But that didn't deter Don Raffaele from putting me on stage again.

On a Sunday early fall afternoon, just before the start of school, the priest came to speak to us at one of our meetings. He gave us the happy news that a big celebration was planned for the Feast of the Rosary. The village's masons had built a new house for the priest and a grotto with a statue of Our Lady of

42

Lourdes outside the church. Under his house, adjacent to the church, would be a theatre, so he could show films all year long. As part of the celebration, a play of the story of Saint Bernadette would be put on to inaugurate both the grotto and the theatre. We spoke with excitement of the plans. He announced that I would be Saint Bernadette. Rosalba, our leader, would play the part of Bernadette's mother.

I walked home with a copy of the play and the feeling that I had been singled out as special. Mother and my neighbours were just as excited as I was. The only thing I was unhappy about was that my father wouldn't see me in the play.

Aurora, who lived in an alley not far from my house, was asked to play the Madonna. She had been chosen because of her long blond hair and gray-blue eyes. Some of the older church ladies snickered when they heard she was playing the part. "Couldn't they have found someone better than the *zingarella*?" they asked.

Aurora's mother, Paola, was a statuesque, fair-haired woman, and was known as a *giruventula*, a busybody, because she went from house to house chattering with people, saying anything that came to her mind. Paola and her husband Micu had met in Cassino after the war. When he brought her to the village, she was already his wife, married in a civil ceremony. Some people doubted they had married at all. They speculated that he had found her in the street and she had just hung on to him for lack of a better life. Why would a good-looking woman like that settle for a taciturn and almost illiterate peasant, if not because she was spoiled goods and needed a roof over her head?

Paola's reputation as a harebrained outsider was sealed when she named her first-born daughter Aurora, instead of Giuseppa, after her father-in-law – an affront to both her husband's family and village traditions. Paola refused to give the delicate bundle of light a name derived from a man's name. She chose Aurora instead, just because she liked its meaning – dawn.

Lucia and Tina made fun of Aurora for having accepted the part. "Isn't she a little too old to be in a play?" Lucia chortled one day at the seamstress's shop.

Aurora shrugged, turning cold toward her two friends. Alfonso had spread rumours that Aurora had flirted with Totu, but Lucia hadn't paid any attention to it, since her brother had tried in various ways before to find fault with both Totu and Aurora.

We rehearsed for weeks, learning the life story of Bernadette Soubirous, a French shepherdess who had lived a hundred years before our time. The girls in the shop had fun dressing me up. With my square face in a flowered scarf, a long skirt, and a red apron, I looked like a real peasant. They twirled me around and laughed at how I looked like a little woman. Aurora had the seamstress, Giovanna, order white satin fabric for her long dress and a wide blue sash.

Don Raffaele told us about Bernadette leading a poor and simple life; yet the Blessed Virgin chose to appear to her in a grotto, in a golden-coloured cloud, and revealed many important things to her. For a period of six months, Bernadette had eighteen apparitions. People were skeptical and persecuted Bernadette and her family. "I do not promise you happiness in this world, but in the next," the Lady said during one of her apparitions.

As Our Lady, Aurora didn't have very many lines. Most of my lines were with the mother, who tried to convince Bernadette to disavow what she had seen, for fear that others would think her crazy. But Bernadette persisted in believing in the visions. She didn't want to forget what the Lady told her, so on one occasion she brought a pencil and paper to write down her words. The Lady told her, "What I have to say does not have to be written down. Open your heart to the message of love."

In one of the most important scenes, the ninth apparition, the Lady asked Bernadette to dig a hole in the ground, to drink the water and bathe in it. I had to pretend to dig, and then I splashed water from a pot on my face. As I acted this part out, I closed my eyes and imagined the stream – a rivulet of clear running water hidden in the underbrush – where my mother and I used to stop on our way to the mountain looking for wood. We drank by cupping water into our hands.

On the water's edge, in spring, I'd find tiny sweet-smelling violets, and, on hot summer days, we would cool our feet in the brook. In Lourdes, the priest said, the watering hole turned into a spring with healing powers, attracting millions of pilgrims.

I had no problem memorizing my lines but I did have to be repeatedly told to raise my voice. Some of the church ladies would sit in the last row of the theatre and call out for me to speak clearly and loudly.

We had been rehearsing together for three weeks when, one day, Aurora didn't show up. Don Raffaele explained that the ladies had decided it would be more effective to have a real statue of Our Lady on stage, and to have one of the women stand behind it and recite the lines. I felt sorry for Aurora, who was very upset when I saw her at the seamstress's shop. She still had to pay for the fabric for the white dress, which was only half finished.

"This village is full of jealous vipers," she said, tears welling in her eyes.

A few days later, Aurora was rushed to the hospital in Catanzaro, where she stayed for a week. Rumours flew about why she had to stay for so long.

"I hope it's not because of the play or the dress," Giovanna said. "I didn't charge for my time cutting it and basting it, but I had to charge her for the fabric."

"Aurora has had other things on her mind besides the play," one of the church ladies replied. "Good thing

46

we thought of the statue. Imagine having someone like her play the part of the Virgin Mary."

The ladies then decided that, during the first apparitions, the statue would remain covered by a veil. When it came time for the final scene, the people in the play knelt in front of the covered statue.

I spoke in a clear voice: "What is your name?"

"I am the Immaculate Conception," the statue replied gravely. The veil dropped and a light shone on the statue of Our Lady of Lourdes. Everyone gasped.

For the ending, Don Raffaele told everyone that Bernadette had entered a monastery, where she lived in humility and prayer till her death. "The saint of Lourdes was the saint of penance and the saint of prayer. She is a shining model for all girls. She was a modest and simple peasant who, through faith, achieved the highest level that is granted to anyone. She became a saint."

Backstage, one of the church ladies planted a wet kiss on my cheek. "*Bravissima, Caterinuccia.* I had goose bumps when the veil came down." From then on, until I left for Canada, whenever I walked by, people would say, "Here comes Saint Bernadette." Had I stayed in Mulirena, that would have been my nickname for the rest of my life.

Whether it was the result of my father's petition, or because there was a surplus of teachers, or simply because it was meant to be, when school started in October, my fourth-grade class was surprised by the appearance of a new male teacher, Signor Gavano from Piemonte. He was a gentle man who came all the way from near the French border to teach in our out-of-the-way village, the name of which was not even on the map of Calabria. A surplus of teachers had been a problem in Italy for ages, so this was not unusual. He left his wife and family behind and boarded at the home of Don Cesare, one of the few homes in the village with running water and a regular bathroom.

On the first day of school, he asked us to bring him the last year's composition notebooks and, when he saw they were mostly blank, he told us that from then on, we'd have to write a composition assignment every week. He also arranged for my class to correspond with another fourth-grade class from his home town, Alessandria, so now we all had pen pals with whom to exchange letters and pictures.

Both these new tasks pleased me. They gave me the idea to fill notebooks with the tidbits of information about people and events in the village I had been collecting in my head all summer. I wrote them down as if I were talking to my pen pal in Piemonte, who knew nothing of our village. For years afterwards, in Montreal, I would pretend to be speaking to my pen pal, as if needing to explain to her the place I lived in and the things I did.

"The Flat, Fertile Farmlands of the Po Valley" was the heading of a magazine article that our new teacher passed around one day, with pictures of gigantic sprinklers used for irrigation. This lesson remains imprinted in my memory, particularly because when I read about the large sprinklers they seemed unreal to me. I had never even seen a small one. Also, I had a first-hand account of someone from another region of Italy, which seemed like a foreign country.

After the lesson, our teacher gave us time to write a composition on Mulirena and the farmlands around it. We would be sending the compositions to our new pen pals so that they in turn would learn about our region.

This is what I wrote:

Dear Maria Rosa,

My baptismal name is Caterina. I'm Catarina or Catarí to my family and Catarinella to older friends and relatives, who use it as a term of endearment. We don't like using our Italian names between us. The one vowel change turns the name into dialect and makes it sound less pretentious.

I don't particularly like my name or its variations, and I especially dislike being called Caterinuccia by our neighbour, Donna Rachele, and by the ladies who work at church and pretend to speak a better Italian than anyone else. I've recently asked my friends to call me Rina, short for Caterina and the original name of my village, Migliarina.

The farmlands around Mulirena are far from fertile or flat. The village itself is a huge hill surrounded by other hills. Except for the potted plants on balconies, there is very little greenery in the village itself. It seems that every inch of space has been covered in stone by the village's *muratori*, stones that shine white in the summer sun, and burn your feet, but turn grey and damp in winter. Mulirena is one huge house. In fact, there are no lawns or fences separating one home from the other. Each house is attached to the others and, because of the elevation, the roofs of some homes are at the same level as the front entrances of others. If ever anyone forgets a key, all we have to do is jump from a neighbour's rooftop onto a balcony and a window.

In Mulirena, my world centers on the school and the parish church. Walking uphill from this church, one reaches the upper outskirts of the village. The wide dirt road, flanked by rows of tall cypresses, leads to the Calvario, a hill with three crosses, the cemetery, and the aqueduct. Because the aqueduct is at the centre of a large grassy field, the kindergarten kids and the summer day-campers often go there on picnics, walking in neat rows, all wearing blue cotton uniforms and starched white caps and singing songs in unison.

This is also the road that leads to the only piece of land that belongs to my mother, a small portion of the highest mountain in the area, dense with chestnut trees – ancient trees so tall they seem to touch the sky. In the summer, the walk to the mountain is a hot trek. But once we arrive, it's the shadiest, coolest, and most peaceful place on earth. On our way up to this land, we always stop by the brook to splash cool water on our faces. Then, while Mother picks chestnuts, gathers kindling, or looks for mushrooms, my brother and I play out the clashes between Roman gladiators and Christians that we've watched in Quo Vadis.

Besides the chestnuts, which are the area's most plentiful produce, and the prized mushrooms, not much else grows on the mountain itself. On its steep sides, some farmers manage to hoe little plots, but irrigation is next to impossible. In the flatter farms that have a shallow river, a Fiumara, flowing through or nearby, they use a very rudimentary system of irrigation. The river water, when it is not dried out in the summer, is diverted, channelled, and contained in huge cement vats.

51

The water from these vats is distributed sparingly, when necessary, through furrows in the soil, and directed toward the orchards. I often watch how carefully my Nanna unblocks a hole in the vat to let out the water, and then guides it lovingly through the furrows, as though she were spoon feeding a feverishly thirsty child.

Because this water has to travel through different farmlands, some fierce battles are fought over the right to use it. Relatives, even brothers and sisters who often share connecting farms, have been known to come to blows and even kill each other over this precious lifeline.

I wish that one day we, too, will have the same gigantic sprinklers with the gyrating flow of water that will keep our farmlands dewy and nourished like the rich green farmlands of Lombardia and Piemonte.

Your new friend,
Caterina/Rina

I had decided to change my name after hearing the story of how Mulirena got its name. Where did the founders get enough sand to build a village, I wondered. The few times I had gone down to the river with my mother, its bed was dry and rocky. The only sandy area I could think of was at the Timpa, but its sand was more like a fine dust that blew over the ravine and dispersed into the air. I tried to imagine teams of women in sixteenth-century costumes – for surely it was the women who were relegated to this chore – trying to gather the fine grains of sand and contain them in sacks to carry away on their donkeys or their heads for men to make stones.

My friends made a feeble attempt at calling me Rina, but not enough for the new name to catch on.

I understood the concept of Signor Gavano's sprinklers only later, when, during my first summer in Montreal, I first saw those crazy little grass sprinklers that turned wildly, spewing water on the lawns around my neighbourhood.

One of Signor Gavano's accomplishments was to research the history of the village's early development, with the help of the village priest. They painstakingly searched the church registers, inventories, records of visits by bishops, and the diocese archives in Nicastro. Years later, they published all this information in a book entitled *The Two Bell Towers of Mulirena,* which was sent to all the Mulerinesi who had left. When my mother received her copy in Montreal, I remember reading it from cover to cover, imagining my teacher from Piemonte and Don Raffaele poring over old papers to piece together a fascinating story that tied the village to Spanish kings and Sicilian counts. The book was then relegated to the old trunk on one of our many moves, and remained there until now.

As the book states, a more political and social perspective to the village's history is unfortunately unavailable, as a suspicious fire at the town hall in July 1933 destroyed many important documents. This would make a fine story at some other time. If told, it might reveal the power that some old families still maintained in the village at that turbulent turning-point in the history of modern Italy.

As far back as 1595, Bishop Pietro Montuoro, after a visit to the area, wrote five lines in Latin that refer to Mulirena, then named Migliarina, as a *casale*, an enclave of rustic farm homes.

In casale Migliarinae una tantum parochialis ecclesia non consecrata sub Sanctue Luciae invocatione invenitur. Eius parochus de Fatio, curatus solus ibi est presbiter. Incolentes 570.

This report confirms that, at the time, there existed one parish church non-consecrated with the name of Santa Lucia, that the pastor's name was de Fabio, and that the village inhabitants totalled 570.

Early church documents included censuses of people and houses. Three classes of people are mentioned: titled *dons* of aristocratic families, *mastri* or tradespeople, and peasants called *villani*. This last term for the proletariat had disparaging connotations even at the time.

Isolated from the rest of the world by geography and the lack of good roads, Mulirena functioned largely in the feudal-like system of its early origins until the Second World War. The territory was owned by absentee landlords from the Kingdom of Naples. In 1601, Mulirena, along with the surrounding territory of present-day Tiriolo and Gimigliano, were sold to Count Carlo Cicala, of Genovese origin and living in Messina, Sicily, for 80,000 ducats. In 1630, he was given the title of Prince of Tiriolo by King Ferdinand IV of Naples. Prince Carlo was succeeded by his son Giovanbattista, who in turn had two sons: Carlo, who died without descendents, and Cesare, whose son Giovanbattista had a son Carlo, who had a son Cesare, and so on and so on.

Feudalism in the kingdom of Naples would only be abolished by law in August, 1806. The name of a descendent of Prince

Carlo-Luigi Cicala, seventh Prince of Tiriolo and Duke of Gimigliano – appears in the
official documents of the period.

Even before compiling the book with these historical facts, Signor Gavano had provided enough pre-
liminary information in class to let my own imagination soar. It was especially fascinating for me to make
the connection between the name of our square and
Don Cesare Cicala, our pharmacist and a descendent
of the sixteenth-century landlord, Prince Carlo Cicala. The hostility between Lucia's and Don Cesare's
family felt even more intriguing once I knew that both
were descendants of a prince.

Lucia's mother, Rosaria Abiusi, was a first cousin to Don Cesare. The resemblance between the two
cousins was striking; she was short and stout, with
curly reddish-brown hair and flushed cheeks, a femi-
nine version of Don Cesare, who was only slightly tall-
er and whose wiry hair was redder than hers. I always
remember her fanning her face with an embroidered
cotton handkerchief. Don Cesare also always carried a
white handkerchief to wipe his sweaty forehead.

The resemblance was only physical; she was far
from enjoying the same wealth and prestige he did.
Her house still belonged to Don Cesare, and Rosaria
had to pay a small yearly rent. Ancestral houses were

generally inherited by first-born sons. Daughters, and especially daughters of daughters, were destined to be short-changed.

The relationship between the cousins had been strained for as long as I could remember. Don Mario Abiusi, Rosaria's husband, had been welcomed into the family because of his title, though his family had become impoverished by the time of his marriage. He became a thorn in the Cicala family's side because he changed his political leanings before the war. The Cicala family and all of Piazza Don Carlo and the upper part of the village had traditionally been staunch Christian Democrats; Don Mario had aligned himself with the ruling Fascist Party and became one of the leaders of a clique of henchmen who were considered thugs by his Christian Democrat in-laws.

Don Cesare and Don Mario only spoke to each other at political speeches, and only to throw insults at each other. Luckily, Don Cesare was hardly ever at home, and Don Mario, half paralyzed since the war, rarely went out of the house.

During one heated speech, Don Cesare, red in the face with rage, with outstretched arms, shouted from the balcony of the town hall balcony, waving his white handkerchief as he spoke. "They forced themselves into our homes at night, shoved castor oil down my father's throat. They pulled off his whiskers until his skin bled raw."

The political animosity between Don Cesare and Rosaria's husband, Don Mario, only widened an already existing rift between the two families.

Though lands and ancestral houses were generally bequeathed to sons, wealthier families often used parcels of lands as dowries to secure good husbands for their daughters. At marriage, Rosaria Abiusi had inherited a small but prized piece of property from her family. The ownership of this small piece of flat land near the river, the *Fiumarella*, had caused fighting between Don Cesare's and Rosaria's families for generations, because the water from the river had to pass through this property to get to the larger orchards inherited by Don Cesare.

Before the war, Don Cesare's father had used families of indentured labourers to look after his lands, while Don Cesare studied in Bologna and became a pharmacist. The pharmacy hardly gave Don Cesare enough to live on. As more peasants abandoned the land to emigrate, Don Cesare became drawn to farming, and only worked at the pharmacy on call. He married a woman from Amato, Donna Rachele Scalise, whose family had also fallen on hard times before the war. She brought with her a brother, Gennaro, and his son, Antonio, to live in a wing of the mansion. The transposed family was rarely called by their proper names but nicknamed *I l'Amatisi*, the people from Amato, and they were treated like foreigners. I don't remember anyone, including his own family, referring to Antonio by any other name but Totu, the dialect diminutive of his given name.

His father, who was always called *U l'Amatise*, was a tall, quiet, educated man whose wife died of tuberculosis when Totu was an infant. He became totally devoted to Don Cesare and his land, and was hardly ever seen in the village; he slept in the *casale*. Together with Don Cesare he found more modern means of managing the olive groves. They installed large nets under every olive tree, which meant they needed fewer labourers to pick olives, and they paid those who worked in cash rather than with a few jugs of oil, while the Abiusi's olives rotted on the ground. They also found a market for the remnants of the dried-up, crushed olives and pits, which came out of the press looking like large cartwheels of cork. *U l'Amatise* was directly responsible for developing this profitable part of the olive oil business. He sold the by-product in the cities, where it was processed and used for fuel. While he worked tirelessly for Don Cesare, Totu was pampered by Donna Rachele and Don Cesare, who were childless.

Don Cesare made money in whatever way he could and did not let pride get in the way. He used the small truck he drove around the village as a taxi service. He charged a minimal amount to drive people to the city when he had to go there for his own dealings. Each summer, he bought out fruit trees from those families who had abandoned them and sold the fruit to vendors in Catanzaro. He planned on doing the same with the fresh vegetables grown in his orchards, but the sharing of the water with the Abiusi family created constant conflict. Since none of the Abiusi children worked the land, and Rosaria only maintained a small vegetable patch, Don Cesare offered to buy out their unused plots, just so he could get to the water, but Alfonso, the eldest son, said he'd rather starve than give up the rights to the water and the land for the benefit of the l'Amatisi.

The jealousy between Don Cesare and his cousin's son, Alfonso, could be traced back to their fathers and to the incident that created an unbridgeable chasm in the village: the fire at the town hall.

"The arrogant bullies who set the fire are still with us, and won't accept the fact they lost the war." That's how Don Cesare spoke about it during his political speeches, which would always end with the sentence, "They shoved castor oil down my father's throat and plucked his whiskers until his skin bled raw."

Don Cesare's father had consistently refused to get a membership card for the Fascist party. Don Mario Abiusi was one of the mayor's men who went around at night and forced castor oil down the throats of those who still resisted the Fascist movement – and who reported any hint of criticism of the party.

One evening in July 1933, the town hall went up

in flames. The church bells rang in alarm at about 10 p.m., and the whole village rushed to watch the building burn. The flames were uncontrollable and completely destroyed the building. The story told in our neighbourhood was that a group of women returning from the farms at dusk saw the mayor's men walking around the building. The women later accused the men of dousing the building with gasoline, but this could never be proven. In the early morning hours, after everyone had gone to bed, those same men stormed into the homes of those who were considered enemies of the *fascio* and arrested them for having set the fire. Don Mario Abiusi was the witness who sent the men into exile for months. He declared that he had heard the stubborn man, Cicala, swear, "Italians should all burn their town halls in protest, if that *cornuto* of Mussolini doesn't stop talking about war and raising our taxes."

Though over two decades had gone by since this incident, old wounds were reopened at every election period, with accounts of the fire and its consequences rehashed by all sides. The village split into two camps: the Christian Democrat mayor, supported by Don Cesare, and the former Fascist mayor, who flip-flopped between different parties. The Fascist party had been outlawed since the end of the war, and its members made convenient affiliations with any of the other lawful parties that opposed the Christian Democrats.

Don Cesare was actively involved with the province's Christian Democratic Party. He spoiled his nephew Totu as his own son. He paid for his studies and openly discussed his plans for a political career for the young man. Alfonso Abiusi, and to a lesser degree his younger brother, Giacomo, opposed with a passion that bordered on hatred whatever political aspirations Don Cesare harboured for himself or his wife's nephew. Don Cesare's business association with *U l'Amatise* also infuriated Alfonso. He couldn't stomach that an upstart from Amato, whose family had had nothing before the war, now ran the land that was part of his family's history, and was making money from it too. Out of spite, Alfonso ridiculed Totu whenever he could, referring to him scornfully as *l'amatu signurinu l'amatise,* the loved little lord from Amato, even though the gentle-mannered man had been his sister Lucia's first and only boyfriend in Mulirena.

Part II

I have been exploring ideas for a love story. "Write what you know" is the usual recommendation in the books on writing I've consulted and the workshops I've attended. I want to set a story in a Calabrian village, a world both familiar to me and at the same time exotic to Canadian readers.

Lucia and Totu's story has never quite left me, but I witnessed it as a child and I don't trust my memories. There are many missing pieces and gaps that need to be filled. I prod my mother. I speak to her as if she were still here, for her voice and words reverberate constantly in my mind.

"In those villages, we fought like cats and dogs. We lived on top of each other. What could you expect?"

It was like her to see the bigger picture, to look beyond what people did to explain why they did it.

"I need to know more about Lucia and Totu,

about their families, their thoughts," I tell myself, "not the whole village."

"You can't speak of one without the other."

She is right, as always.

Tina's boyfriend, Michele, left for Rome at the beginning of September to work as a tailor. Saverio, Aurora's boyfriend, was called for his military service in Bari. Totu was the only one who remained in the village. He had expected to go to university in Rome, but his uncle convinced him that it was more important to stay close to home and build up connections in the provincial city. In the end, Don Cesare believed it would be those friendships that would get Totu a position in Calabria, not the degree. Lucia said that Totu had agreed to become an accountant only for the sake of staying closer to her.

Totu travelled back and forth between Mulirena and Catanzaro, where he studied, and helped his father with deliveries. Whenever he could, he walked by Lucia's window during the day and joined his friend *U Grancu* at his house at night

The girls didn't go to the Funtanella as often because the water from the aqueduct was more plentiful, and the weather had become wet and drab.

Before leaving, Michele had gone to Tina's house to ask *U Grancu*, her older brother, for her hand. After her family in Montreal was informed of the visit, the two became officially engaged. With her boyfriend gone, Tina didn't go out as frequently. It wasn't considered proper for an engaged girl to go out on the *passeggiate* and be seen roaming around the village. Aurora had decided that she didn't want to have anything more to do with Saverio.

"You can't go from one boyfriend to another," Tina warned Aurora. "People are talking."

Aurora stopped sleeping at Don Cesare's house in the fall after she returned from the hospital, and then the "voices" really started. I always found it curious that people referred to village gossip as "voices," as though vicious rumours were started and spread by some faceless force from the sky. In the play, the voices that Bernadette claimed to hear came from the sky, and the villagers made fun of her.

Even before the play, Aurora had begun to develop a reputation as being too "free," and Alfonso kept on spreading the gossip that she spent too much time at *U Grancu*'s house late at night, especially when Totu was there, and who knew what she and Totu did when Aurora slept at Don Cesare's house as a child. Tina defended Aurora, confirming that the girl had only gone to her house to deliver fruit and vegetables from the farm, but Alfonso didn't believe her. Alfonso also claimed that Totu and Aurora spent too much time together at Don Cesare's farm. After that, there were many angry looks and words exchanged from the balcony between Lucia and Totu, and many exchanges of letters.

In his letters, Totu assured Lucia that there was nothing between him and Aurora, and even Aurora swore to Lucia on the head of her youngest brother that she had always considered Totu as another brother, and Totu only went to the farm on account of his uncle's business. Things cooled between Lucia and Aurora, but they were still speaking to each other. Then Aurora was suddenly removed from the Saint Bernadette play, and she did something that had the whole village talking. Who could stop the voices then?

After Mass, on a Sunday, Aurora raided Don Cesare's medicine cabinet and swallowed a bottle of pills. A hysterical Donna Rachele alarmed the whole neighbourhood when she found Aurora in a daze and the empty pill bottle on the floor. Don Cesare made Aurora vomit and carried her like a rag doll down to the piazza and into his truck. When she returned home from the city's hospital, looking pale and gaunt, the story that came out was that she had been found to be pregnant, and that Don Cesare had arranged for an abortion.

Two days after her return, her father, on a drinking binge, was heard yelling outside the *osteria*. "My hunting rifle is ready for *U Grancu* and his lazy, good-for-nothing friends."

That same week, Totu suddenly left for Rome to enroll at the university, even though he had started classes in Catanzaro a month earlier. I saw the note

Totu sent to Lucia. "You're as much of a cretin as the others to believe these malicious rumours," it said. Lucia tore the note to shreds. She couldn't understand the sudden departure, and what she found most suspicious was that, if Aurora had really been pregnant, she had never told her two friends. They were still close, and they used to tell each other everything – especially Aurora, who was so frank and open. When Aurora came back from the hospital, she never denied anything.

"If she did it," Lucia said, "she did it out of envy, and if she didn't do it, she refuses to deny it out of envy too." After Totu's departure, the girls never spoke again.

With Totu in Rome, Don Cesare went back and forth between Aurora's and her former boyfriend's parents, negotiating as only he could. Aurora's former boyfriend, Saverio, was still in Bari when all this happened but, by the end of the month, he came home on leave, and he and Aurora were married in a subdued and quiet wedding early on a Sunday morning before Mass. The priest wouldn't marry Aurora in a white dress, and her family didn't insist on it – proof to everyone that the stories about her pregnancy were true. She wore the little yellow suit she had worn at Easter with a white shawl over it. Don Cesare, Donna Rachele, and Signor Gavano were the only ones to attend the wedding ceremony aside from the two families. Don Cesare and Signor Gavano signed the marriage register as witnesses and then went home. The bride and groom had Sunday lunch with their families at Aurora's house. After lunch, Domenico went back to work at the oil press, and Aurora, Saverio, and his family walked to the far end of the village where they lived. The next day, the groom went back to complete his military service, while the bride remained with his family.

Another commotion was created at Tina's house a few weeks later when Michele wrote from Rome to break their engagement. He said he felt too young to be engaged, that he had to think of his future first.

"It's all excuses," Mother said. "He found himself a *Romana*."

"But we were engaged," Tina cried.

Luckily there had never been any reproaches about Tina's behaviour with Michele, so it was likely that she would find another boyfriend in Mulirena, but, just the same, the break-up, after the official engagement, felt like a blow to the family's honour. Tina would be better off immigrating to Montreal to start afresh. Her elderly parents didn't work and they were dependent on her older brother there, but he didn't yet have enough money to sponsor her.

"How could someone change so quickly?" Tina asked Lucia.

After barely a month of living in Rome, Totu also sent Lucia a letter. She read and reread it out loud, trying to understand what it really meant: "I still love you," it said. "But the gods are not with us right now. I need to give my studies my fullest attention."

"Does that mean he's leaving me for good?" she asked crying. Then he stopped writing.

Mother was in a foul mood when she heard the news about Totu and Lucia. "You'd think these men have never seen women when they go away, and get bamboozled by the first city *zingara* they meet."

The *passeggiate,* the love letters, the stolen glances, the whispered promises turned into memories. It seemed as if suddenly all the men had either broken their pledges or given up on them. They had all but disappeared from our lives. The rain that started pouring from the grey November skies drenched the air of the Piazza of Love with the sadness of the women's tears.

December would have been a dismal month in Mulirena if it hadn't been for the feast of Santa Lucia. It was celebrated on the thirteenth with a three-day fair during which the village was overrun by pilgrims, merchants and gypsies. The piazza outside the upper church, which was named after Santa Lucia, was transformed into a market with stalls selling everything from pots and pans and earthenware to ribbons and special sweets. The market ran all the way up to the Calvario, where farmers met to sell and buy livestock. The squeals of pink piglets being held tightly around the waist as they were carried home were heard throughout the three days, since almost everyone in the village bought a baby hog to fatten and slaughter the following February. People waited all year for the fair to buy new braziers, copper pots, clay water jugs, and hard biscuits – *mustaccioli* and *susumelle* – to eat at Christmas.

A few people came to show their devotion to the Saint, to repay graces received, or to make special vows, especially if they suffered from eye problems, as Santa Lucia is the patron saint of eyes and light. The story we learned in Catechism class was that Lucia of Syracuse, an early Christian, had vowed her life to Christ. She rejected an arranged marriage to a pagan bridegroom and, for this reason, she was arrested and persecuted. First, they tried forcing her into prostitution, but when the guards went to get her, they couldn't move her – not even with a team of oxen. They tried lighting a fire around her, but the fire would not catch. They finally succeeded in killing her by stabbing her in the throat with a dagger, after tearing her eyes out of their sockets. But the legend has it that her eyesight was restored just before her death. In statues and holy pictures she is shown carrying two eyeballs on a small platter in her left hand, while in her right, she holds up an olive branch. Santa Lucia is venerated as both a virgin and a martyr.

December started out wet and blustery, and then turned cold. It snowed a few days before the feast. The water in the drainpipes crystallized into icicles around the houses. A light blanket of snow covered the rooftops. Mother reached over Comare Rosaria's rooftop from our kitchen window and filled a bowl with snow. She sprinkled sugar and cold coffee over it to make *scirubetta* for me, Luigi, and my desk-friend, Bettina, who came over every afternoon to do homework with me. Signor Gavano gave us lots of homework.

Mortified and inconsolable since their boyfriends abandoned them, Lucia and Tina rarely went out anymore. Tina blamed and cursed Rome for her misfortune; Lucia blamed Mulirena and its wagging tongues.

A caravan of vendors came into the village a few days before the fair to set up their stalls. They had to be accommodated in homes since there were no inns. The church remained open for people who had nowhere else to sleep. Many vendors had established friendships in the village over the years, and made sleeping arrangements there. A family of merchants, two brothers and their mother, from Serra San Pietro, a village located high in the mountains, stayed at Lucia's house. They sold aluminum pots and pans, and their dialect was rough and their manners unpolished, despite the fact that the brothers had lived in America before the War. They had made some money before returning to Italy to set up their businesses. They had bought olive oil from the Abiusi, and Alfonso had had other dealings with them. A third brother, Pasquale, had remained in Canada and, according to them, was making a fortune as a contractor in Montreal. He was still single, in his early thirties. His mother told Comare Rosaria that Pasquale didn't want to have anything to do with the girls there; even the Italian girls who had settled in Montreal were too modern for him. *Moglie e buoi dai paesi tuoi* was an old saying in Italy; it meant that wives and oxen are best chosen in one's own village. On their first evening in the village, Alfonso was seen arguing and negotiating with the two brothers at the local *osteria* until late at night, his usual style of conducting business.

Visitors to the fair who did not need accommodation were the gypsies. Arriving in large numbers, they camped out in the open fields, sleeping in make-shift tents, doorways, or on the bare church floor. The women wore long skirts, colourful scarves with fringes, dangling earrings, and shining gold necklaces. They carried dirty babies on their hips and went around the village asking for money. In exchange, they would tell fortunes, remove evil spells – the *malocchio* – or curse you. Some people used their services, but no one trusted them. Household items mysteriously went missing when some gypsy visited. Mother didn't believe in the evil eye or the gypsies' magical powers to predict the future.

"If they know how to tell fortunes, why don't they improve on their own, instead of going around begging?" she used to say.

I was especially intrigued by how they lived. You couldn't tell who was married to whom. They spoke

74

a funny Italian and, among themselves, an incomprehensible language.

"Where do they come from?" I wanted to know. But no one ever seemed to know the answer. "Where do they go from here?" Nobody knew.

On the first day of the fair, gypsies passed by Piazza Don Carlo, shouting, "Pots soldered like new." A young girl, about my age, held a baby on her hip. She smiled, waved at me. I wanted to talk to her, to ask her about school and about where she lived, but Mother shooed them off. She admonished me, as she did each chance she got: "It's better not to start talking to them. They have their ways. They'll make you believe that day is night, night is day. You'll never win with the *zingari*."

The following day, my friend Bettina and I were sitting on her doorstep, looking at one of her older brother's books, a thick novel, *I Promessi Sposi*, that everyone in Italy studied in high school. The young gypsy with the child sneaked up on us.

"*Ciao*. What are your names? Mine is Maria."

We introduced ourselves. "Where do you come from?" I asked. She shrugged and asked if she could look at the book. While leafing through it, she asked if we would be going to the fireworks the following night.

"Yes, do you want to come with us?" I asked.

Maria answered quickly that she'd join us. She said we should wait for her on the road across from the

Timpa just before the fireworks started. She then asked if she could borrow the book for the day.

"It's my brother's," Bettina told her. "I can't give it to you."

"I don't want to keep it, just look at it. I'll bring it back tomorrow at the fireworks. But if you want it before, come and see me at the aqueduct, where I'm staying."

"We can pick it up when we go to the fair, after Mass," I said, looking at Bettina. Maria was off with the book before Bettina could answer.

"What will I tell my brother when I get home?" Bettina asked.

"Tell him you lent it to me," I said.

The morning after, on the day of the feast, Bettina came by my house early. She said she wanted to go to the aqueduct before Mass, to get her book back. "It's your fault," she told me. "You got too friendly with her. I don't think she can even read. She'll probably sell it at the fair."

"We'll get it. Don't worry."

Vendors were busy setting up their stalls for the busiest day of the fair. We walked past pigs, chickens and donkeys for sale. Farmers inspected the animals, haggling over prices. The family from Sierra San Pietro was busy laying out their pots and pans on a table, while Alfonso, in a new suit, leaned across the table and spoke animatedly with the brothers.

Wearing new woolen dresses, long, thick stockings, and ankle-high shoes, we walked to the aqueduct, near the cemetery, where a band of gypsies had camped out. There too, a gypsy was negotiating with a farmer over a donkey; others were sitting soldering old copper pots, while some women nursing babies stretched out their hands whenever someone passed by them.

Maria, holding the same child she had carried the first day we saw her, sat next to the man who was selling the donkey. The farmers took a wad of money, counted it, and passed it to the gypsy, who then passed it to Maria. She counted the money and nodded to the farmer. He took the donkey by the reins and walked away, smiling.

As we approached her, Bettina told Maria, "I want my book."

"I'll bring it to you at the fireworks. I told you already."

"My brother wants it this morning," Bettina said.

"I don't have it. I lent it to my friend."

"You told us we could come and get it anytime we wanted."

"How can I give it to you if I don't have it?"

"Where's your friend?"

"She had to go to Amato with her father to buy a donkey. But she'll be back this afternoon. Wait for me before the fireworks. I told you already."

We had no choice but to leave without the book,

and to join our mothers at church for High Mass. We didn't tell them that we had walked all the way to the aqueduct by ourselves.

After Mass, Comare Rosaria invited Mother and me to her house before lunch to have a drink in celebration of Lucia's name day. She served us a glass of homemade sweet yellow liqueur, which tasted like *Strega,* and some almond cookies. Lucia seemed animated but distracted, as though something was on her mind.

"Lucia has found a nice boyfriend," Comare Rosaria said, as though she were making fun of her.

"Don't you start telling everyone about a boyfriend," Lucia said, sounding annoyed and leaving the room.

Comare Rosaria explained that, the previous evening, Lucia had consented to consider an engagement to her guests' brother from Canada. Comare Rosaria, at first, was not excited about the proposal, because of the age difference, but the brothers convinced them that Pasquale was a serious, hardworking man who had built his own business. He also owned a house and a car. Lucia would live like a lady there, and wouldn't need to go to work, unlike many women who emigrated. Alfonso had negotiated all the details in favour of his sister. Pasquale would pay all the expenses related to the wedding and the trip. After listening to her brother's arguments, Lucia agreed to correspond with the man and to send him her picture, but she would make the final decision only after meeting Pasquale in person, in the summer, when he was expected to visit his family.

"If it's destined, it will happen," Mother said.

"He seems serious and settled, not like these young men around here who don't know what they want," Comare Rosaria explained. "In a few years, she can sponsor her brothers in America. There's nothing for them here."

"Then maybe we'll all be in Montreal one day. You too, Comare Rosaria," Mother said.

"Let's not put the cart before the horse," Lucia, who had been listening from the other room, said. "I won't have an official engagement until I see him."

Comare Rosaria whispered, "In the last months she's become like a ghost. She doesn't eat or talk to anyone. At least this man will keep his word."

"Don't worry. She's young and has a life ahead of her," Mother said.

Then Comare Rosaria held up the picture of a small man sitting on the hood of a big white car, his teeth white and large against his suntanned, bony face.

When we got home, Mother said, "I can't imagine Lucia married to that man."

At the fireworks, there was no sign of Maria. Bettina was upset and cried. She was expecting a good spanking from her brother.

Rosaria and Lucia were accompanied by their

house guests. People kept congratulating both Lucia and the woman from Serra San Pietro.

"It's hard to keep things secret in this village," Comare Rosaria whispered to my mother. "The family gave her a gold necklace and bracelet, and they want some guarantees before leaving that she's as serious as they are, so, unofficially, they're engaged."

The morning after, as the village was emptying of its visitors, I walked with Bettina to the aqueduct. Maria's family was nowhere to be seen. Bettina cried again, but her problem seemed small compared to that of the farmer who had bought the donkey the day before. He was cursing and screaming at the remaining gypsies because they couldn't tell him where to find the man who had sold him the animal. His new donkey had disappeared during the night while he was at the fireworks.

When they heard the stories down at Piazza Don Carlo from the postman who delivered the afternoon mail, they all made fun of us girls for lending something to a gypsy and expecting to get it back, and they especially laughed at the farmer who had bought a donkey from a gypsy and then left it unattended.

In spite of what happened, I felt sorry for Maria.

"Do you think that Maria ever goes to school?" I asked Mother.

"Maria who?"

"The gypsy with the baby."

"How can she go to school, poor girl, when her

parents drag her from village to village with that baby stuck to her hip while they go begging for work? It's not a life for anyone."

"Is it possible that after all these years no one knows where the gypsies go?" I pressed my mother, again.

"You're really hard-headed," Mother said impatiently, folding the letter she had just received from father. "They're *zingari!* How can I explain it to you? They're people without a home. That's why we call them *zingari*."

I pulled the letter from my mother's hands.

Montreal, 12/13, 1955
Cara Teresa,

It has been three months already since I left. I can't tell you how much I miss you and the children. My health is good and I hope that you and everyone else are also fine. Here, we're buried in snow. The days are short, but still too long for me. Construction stops in the winter, and I have no work. I spend the day reading the newspaper, walking around the house, playing with my nephew, and helping my sister cook dinner. By four in the afternoon, it's already dark, and everyone runs home, eats, and gets ready for bed. My poor sister has a house full of men, eight in all, counting her boys, and she never stops

with the washing, ironing, cooking and pre-
paring lunches for us. The little money we
give her for our board hardly pays for all the
food we consume. Sometimes in the afternoons I go to an Italian bar in the hope of
making some contacts and finding work. I've
just made the acquaintance of a Calabrese
who has made lots of money and runs a band
that plays at processions and Italian feasts. I
already played once with them. For me, it's
a good pastime. With Francesco, we're plan-
ning on starting an orchestra to play at Italian weddings. If it works out, we can make
some extra money. I have a lot of company,
and in that sense it's better than living alone
as I did in Milan, but the work here is not
the same. People that tended goats in Italy
have become contractors here. I just got my
card as a bricklayer, but I won't be using it
until next summer. For now, I go begging
for any small repair job I can get. But these
small Italian contractors pay in cash without
declaring me, so I can never collect *shiumag-
giu*, which is what they pay here to those that
don't have work.

Francesco is starting the paperwork to
sponsor Tina. But he's young and has been
spending all his money going out every Sat-

urday night with the French girls. I'll have to lend him a bit of money. I'm doing it for Tina, not for him. She didn't deserve what Michele did to her. Rest assured that I'll make whatever sacrifice to call for you as soon as possible, hopefully by next year. It's the only reason I decided to come here in the first place, to give you and the children a better life. If I can only get through this first winter, then next summer should be easier. With my bricklayer card I get paid up to three dollars an hour, and if I work most of the summer, I'll make enough to rent and furnish an apartment and call for you. I'm still paying the government every month for the loan on the boat trip, and I have to show I have enough to sponsor you. By next year, half of Piazza Don Carlo will be in Montreal.

Give my regards to your family, and don't neglect to take the children to visit my father and mother every Sunday afternoon, and don't be too strict with Luigi. I heard you hung his bicycle from a beam, so he can't reach it. Let him use it once in a while. Tell him I'll buy him a better one when he gets here, and the streets here are all flat. I'm glad that Caterina likes her new teacher. Here, there are parks everywhere, with swings and all kinds of toys for them to play with in the summer, but don't think it's all paradise — winters are long and hard for everyone.

I'm sending you a money order, which should last you till next time I write. Buy the children some candies and oranges for the Befana, and buy my parents some coffee and sugar. Buy three packs of cigarettes and give one to your brother, one to my father, and one to my friend Amadeo, when you see him. Tell him that the band leader here was interned during the war for being a Fascist, and yet the first piece of music that the band plays when we go marching is *Faccetta Nera*. Not only would we be pelted by the Christian Democrats of Piazza Don Carlo, but we would be arrested in Italy for playing it. Here nobody complains. In fact they applaud, and the Canadians smile and don't know any better. I wish I could send more, but whatever I saved has to last until I get regular work again.

Dear Teresa, we're very, very far, and we have to spend Christmas away from each other. I can't even ask you to be with me by looking at the moon every night at ten as I used to from Milan, for when the moon is out here the sun is getting ready to rise over there. I can't wait for this long winter to be over and have you in my arms forever.

Wish everyone a Merry Christmas. Kiss the children for me. With all my love,

Giuseppe

My father was my mother's first and only boyfriend and the only man she ever loved. In the true Calabrian code of behaviour, my parents were never allowed to be alone together until their wedding night, though she admitted to furtive love letters pitched through her window when her father was not around. Theirs was not an arranged marriage.

My mother often spoke of how, before the war and before they were married, my father used to gather his musician friends and serenade her under her balcony. The makeshift band played the same favourite song, *Scrivimi,* night after night, until one night my grandfather, tired of hearing it, threw a pail of hot dishwater out the window and scurried them off.

My mother's father, Gabriele Mancuso, born in the nineteenth century, even before Italy was unified, lost his first wife and then remarried at sixty years of age with a twenty-two year-old widow, and fathered my mother and three other children with her. In spite of this healthy reproductive activity for a man his age, he was a very stern disciplinarian. My mother never complained about the strict moral rules to which she had been subjected as a young woman. In fact she derived a certain sense of security from the old traditions, since they had done her no harm. She had all she wanted out of life – the man she loved, a home in Piazza Don Carlo, and then two beautiful children. But the war spoiled it all. It first took the men away from their families, then caused the devastation that forced the men to wander in all corners of the country begging for work.

It didn't seem to have registered in my mother's consciousness that the state of the economy in southern Italy before the war had been just as dire. She spoke of life before the war with longing. The village was full of young people serenading each other; the young men put on mystery plays during the major religious holidays; a musical band played outdoor concerts regularly; and fairs during the major religious holidays attracted people from all around the area. Walking down alleys in the summer evenings one could hear the laughter of women sitting on doorsteps in groups, and the men who paraded back and forth playing tricks on each other to entertain the women.

Her own family had always been well provided for. Her youthful mother, Stella, was a force of nature, looking after a horde of stepchildren, some older than she, running a bakery, and supervising work in their extensive farmlands while raising her own young brood. My mother's distinguished father sat behind the grocery store counter all day and played court to his friends. He also worked as a tailor, specializing in sewing the heavy pleated skirts and vests used by women for their costumes, a trade practiced by very few tailors in the village. The tradition of the *pacchiana* costume died with them, and so did the pre-war bucolic existence in the village.

I had only heard the broader lines of my mother's particular family history, just as one of the many odd phenomena of life in an insular village at the turn of the century. With my new focus on writing, I now marvel at the many potential love stories to be harvested from those ancient village tales.

One such tale starts like an eighteenth century melodrama, with an abandoned baby, Luigi Anastasia, born in 1897. His father, like many men in the village, had gone to Argentina to work, but unlike the others who returned after amassing a bundle of money, he neither returned nor made any contact with his young wife and baby boy. The wife, out of resentment, desperation and dire straits, took off to Egypt to work as a nursemaid. She couldn't bring the baby with her, so she left him in the care of her mother's elderly cousin. A year, two years passed, and Luigi's mother didn't find her way home. Call it negligence, lack of resources, or just plain egotism – nobody pinned a reason for her extreme forgetfulness – but she never returned for him, and neither did his father. The cousin died. Her husband, also getting on in years, was half blind and couldn't care for the young child indefinitely. A neigbour, Teresa, had married a well-to-do young tailor, landowner and merchant, Gabriele. Teresa had one child after another, six in all, and baby Luigi slipped into her household as one of her own. He lived with her family until his eighteenth birthday, when he became engaged to Caterina. His future brothers-in-law had all emigrated to America, and they encouraged the young man to join them there to work on the building of the Brooklyn Bridge. Luigi had never known hard manual labour. He had taken up the trade of stone mason, but never worked at anything more strenuous than small repair jobs around town – fountains, terraces, cemetery crypts. He couldn't get used to the slave-like conditions in New York's Lower East Side, where the immigrant men lived. Years later, he would say, "They called us dagos and frisked us if we wanted to go in a movie theatre or a bar. But that was before Mussolini came and made the world respect us."

He left New York City for a while to go searching for lighter work at upstate New York farms. He travelled to Canada for a short stint and lived in Montreal. The stories he brought back with him about Canada were all about frozen ears and noses; those about New

York and the Bronx included brawls with Blacks the size of giants and dumb American men in baggy pants and their half-naked women. They were always stories about a living hell made bearable only by the knowledge that he would eventually return to the *paese*.

Much to the chagrin of his more industrious brothers-in-law, he returned to the village as empty-handed as he had left. He found his surrogate mother Teresa dead of typhus, a disease that took many lives in those days. Within the year, his surrogate father Gabriele, already sixty years of age, arranged a marriage for himself with a young widow, Stella, whose husband had died in the war. Luigi and Caterina were married on the same day and at the same mass as Gabriele and Stella.

A year later Luigi had a son, Giuseppe, named after the husband of his mother's cousin who had taken him in as a baby. Not to be outdone, six months later, Gabriele had a daughter and named her Teresa after his first wife. Giuseppe became a mason like his father, learned to play the trumpet, and played in the village band and, as an eighteen year old, started serenading Teresa, right under the balcony of the house where his father had been raised. Giuseppe and Teresa were my father and mother. My mother was the only first-born daughter in town named not after her paternal grandmother, but after her husband's grandmother by adoption. They were not related by blood, but as my mother would put it, they were linked forever by destiny.

My father left Italy reluctantly and with a sense of failure at not being able to make it in his own country. My mother, on the other hand, who never craved the excitement of travel, was happy to emigrate, just so the family could live together in one place. She looked forward to getting a job outside the home. "At least a woman can help the family and not be dependent on her husband," she'd say. She was especially anxious to escape the constant prying of nosy neighbours and the spiteful games some of them played.

Part III

In the summer of 1956, the "voices" around the village were all about Totu and Lucia. At Giovanna's shop, at *U Grancu*'s house, the big question was whether or not the two would find a way of getting back together again.

When Totu came home for a few days at Easter and visited *U Grancu*'s house, he walked right past Lucia's window without looking up. She steamed with anger knowing he was across the way and had made no attempt to see her.

"It's as if I never existed," she complained to her friends at the seamstress's shop. "After all those years, the least I deserve is an explanation."

At the bar, Totu had been heard saying, "War criminals were brought to justice in Nuremberg, but Mario Abiusi and the Fascist thugs of our village are still free. Shame on our political system!"

Lucia spoke more and more about her prospective

fiancé and his impending trip to Mulirena, which would make their engagement official.

He had written to her that he had acquired large plots of land in Montreal that he expected to develop into rows and rows of houses built just like those in the song *Casetta in Canada* everyone around the village was singing.

To Lucia's boasts, Totu responded, "For gain and profit, men sell their souls; women their bodies."

In preparation for being called to Montreal, Tina had a new suit and coat sewn with some money Father had sent her. Mother worried that if Father kept lending money to anyone who needed it, he would never be able to send for us. But in the spring, Father wrote that he had resumed working regularly, and that the proceedings to sponsor Tina were moving ahead quickly. By the beginning of May, Tina went to Rome for her visa and, soon after, left for Montreal.

"It won't be long before Lucia joins Tina in Montreal. What future would she have here, after the way Totu treated her?" the women of Piazza Don Carlo said.

In June, at the end of the school year, Totu came back from Rome again, and a few days later, at the bar, he and his uncle argued in the presence of many of their friends.

"You're a big disappointment!" Don Cesare burst out. "After all I've done for you! My father was exiled and had his whiskers pulled off, one hair at a time, because he wouldn't belong to any political party, and you – my nephew – a Communist! What a slap in the face!"

"It's the only party that cares for workers," Totu replied.

"It's people like me who create jobs that help people. I put bread on their tables, while you and your Communist friends just talk," Don Cesare said.

"Bread maybe, while you eat capicollo and prosciutto," Totu responded.

"What an ingrate! You're studying this nonsense on my back, instead of becoming an accountant or a lawyer and earning a decent living. What are you going to do with a degree in *Lettere* here?"

"I'm going to be a writer," Totu said loudly, making sure that everyone in the bar heard him.

"Another deluded fool with dreams of glory!" Don Cesare laughed. He threw some money on the table and left.

As the summer proceeded, Lucia and her brother Alfonso were heard arguing continually over Pasquale, who did not keep his promise about coming to Mulirena, but just wrote that he had had an unusually busy period at work. He had started selling the plots of land and had a quota to reach before the end of summer. The marriage plans would have to change; they would have to marry by proxy, like many others had done before them.

"I'm not like many others," Lucia complained. "I'm not a peasant who has to marry at any cost."

Alfonso warned her: "You can't break your word with the family. If you do, you're finished. No one will want to touch you here in Mulirena."

Pasquale's family came to visit every Sunday, and Comare Rosaria complained to my mother that she had to force Lucia to be civil with them. Alfonso discussed new business opportunities with Pasquale through his brothers. Pasquale insisted that a fortune could be made importing Italian food products, especially the locally produced ones, such as olive oil, cheeses, and salami.

"American food is garbage," he quoted Pasquale.

Don Cesare laughed when he heard about their plans. He kept on buying up the lands that others abandoned, and produced and bottled olive oil, which he then sold to dealers in the cities. "*Io faccio l'America qui*," he said. He'd make his fortune in Mulirena. A few weeks later he put a banner in front of his mansion, *Evviva l'Italia; Abbasso l'invidia!* – Long live Italy; Down with envy!

Towards the end of the summer, Totu spent more and more time at his friend's courtyard, which overlooked Lucia's window, while Lucia spent her afternoons on her balcony, embroidering her trousseau.

Alfonso travelled in the surrounding areas with a new scooter that Pasquale had paid for. When in the village, he kept a close eye on Totu's comings and goings.

Aurora's husband was still doing his military service, but he was on leave frequently. When Aurora became pregnant, tongues started wagging about the possible identity of the father.

"It's not fair," Giovanna said. "Why don't they leave the poor girl alone? One wrong deed seals a woman's reputation for good here...." She waved her long seamstress's shears. "I'd like to cut their tongues off."

Aurora didn't let the gossip bother her. She stopped going to the seamstress's shop to avoid seeing Lucia, and bought ready-made clothes in Catanzaro instead. On more than one of her excursions, it was Totu who drove her to the city in his uncle's car.

"So you can't deny it now. It's all true what they've said," Lucia wrote in a note that I delivered to Totu. He scribbled back: "What right do you have to question my every movement when you've chosen to sell yourself to a man you don't even know?"

When Lucia received this response, she opened her back window and the whole neighbourhood heard her scream at Aurora who was shelling peas behind Rachele's house, "*Puttana, e figlia de puttana.*"

"Why don't you take your anger out on someone else?" Giovanna yelled at Lucia the following day.

"Who am I going to take it out on?" she answered. "Who will listen to me?"

Giovanna and the other seamstresses agreed. "Aurora is not the problem. It's Totu who doesn't know what he wants."

Meanwhile, Pasquale started proceedings for Lucia to go to Montreal.

One evening, at *U Grancu*'s house, Totu, despondent, confessed to his friends that he'd been a fool to let Lucia slip through his fingers and that he'd do anything to keep Lucia from marrying a stranger.

"It's all talk," Giovanna said.

I noticed Totu coming by Piazza Don Carlo more often, and I was as curious as everyone else.

I sat serenely on my doorstep, in my secluded square, copying poems on a small notepad. I wore a satiny red skirt with pink lace trim at the hem and a white cotton blouse with a Peter Pan collar. My thick, chin-length brown hair was kept neatly off my face with a large pink bow. The air was so still that I could hear, from her window, Lucia's needle pierce the linen fabric held taut in her round embroidering loop, and the buzzing of the flies that circled around us.

I hated those uneventful weekday afternoons after the midday meal, when shopkeepers closed up for the siesta. The slow pace of the village became even slower. Most men were away at work. The village was left with old people, women, children, and aimless young men. The women were not siesta takers. On one late summer afternoon, when the air was beginning to cool, my mother and Comare Rosaria left for the countryside, looking for twigs. This was a daily task for older women.

Though oil lamps had given way to naked light bulbs hanging from ceilings, the hearths for cooking and braziers for heating still had to be fuelled through the tireless energy of the women. I would normally have wanted to tag along to look for wild violets in the woods, but that day I chose to stay behind, in awe of my new clothes and pencils that had arrived from far away the day before. I sat on my doorstep, drawing violets on the cover of the notepad, wanting to make my own poetry book to keep as a souvenir.

Lucia was also home. Young women of the village helped with the house-cleaning, cooking and sewing, but the hard work was relegated to older women. I was left with her, but chose to sit on my doorstep. Totu had started coming this way again almost every day. He was home for the summer from Rome, where he had finished his first year of university. He pinched my cheek as he passed by me, said, "*Ciao,* Caterina," and let out a short whistle. Lucia opened her shutters and peeked out. Totu fixed his gaze on the window and found his customary spot under the door of *U Grancu*'s house. He came when her parents and brother were not home.

Totu asked, "Any news?"

"Nothing yet," answered Lucia. "Why should you care?"

"Maybe we're better off throwing ourselves off the bridge and into the ravine."

"What should I do?" she replied. "I have a family and two brothers on my back. You tell me what to do."

"This place has become a prison."

"Tell me when, and we'll run away," she said.

"I can't wait to get out of here."

They were waiting for a letter. In a village in which practically every family had someone living far away, the sight of Martino, the mailman, was awaited with great anticipation. He delivered mail twice a day: in the early morning and in the late afternoon. The previous day, he had brought my family a notice for a package – a package from America. Mother had an old aunt who had immigrated to Brooklyn in the 1930s. After the war, she sent packages of used clothing: garish satin party dresses, oversized men's underwear. Years later, we would laugh at the thought of those ugly American clothes. But, at the time, we considered ourselves to be the best-dressed kids in the village – and the only ones to wear pajamas. These packages always brought a surprise. We never knew what we would find: a piece of America to discover.

The day before, in the folds of a red satin skirt, a set of colouring pencils and a notepad fell out. The elation I'd felt at such an unexpected gift still had me floating in the clouds. Meanwhile the two lovers, and the rest of the village, were waiting in suspended animation for something from the postman.

The most anticipated piece of mail was a large

envelope from Rome – *l'Atto di Richiamo,* which we called *a chiamata.* The official request to report to Rome to obtain a visa came after a family member had been approved as a sponsor. For many, receiving this letter was comparable to winning a lottery. The fortunes of the whole family were expected to change. We received ours at the end of June, and Zio Pietro had already made the arrangements for us to go to Rome in early September.

Little by little, activity was resuming around the square, and Totu thought it wise to leave. Mother and Comare Rosaria, carrying loads of dried wood on their heads and talking in low voices, made their way toward the house. They carried the wood with straight backs, walking in the slow, resigned gait of the older women in their layers upon layers of heavy clothing.

"What can I say, Comare Teresa?" Comare Rosaria said. "The world is made like this, and there is nothing we can do to change it. We all want the best for our children. Whatever is meant to be, will be."

"We can't change fate. God will provide."

As she passed by me, Comare Rosaria said, "Did Martino pass yet?"

"No, he hasn't passed yet."

The women unloaded their bundles, and Mother offered me a little bouquet of wild violets.

Martino finally arrived with nothing for my family. The smile on his face as he walked toward Comare

Rosaria told us he might have something special for her. She opened the large brown envelope, and shouted in excitement, "*A chiamata! A chiamata! Lucia!*"

News of this latest call soon travelled down the narrow street to the central piazza, where most of the men sipped coffee at the bar or played billiards. The sun turned the sky into a mellow burnt orange. Totu came up the street toward Lucia's house. This time he didn't stop to pinch my cheeks. He let out a short whistle, then a second and then a third, but Lucia's window remained shut. As he passed by me, slouching, I saw his watery eyes. He made me think of a wounded puppy.

My brother Luigi was back from the tailor's shop where he spent every afternoon. Mother called us in for supper. The first church bell had rung, telling people to get ready for the evening benediction and rosary. A second bell would advise us to leave the house. The third bell would announce that the evening service had begun.

At the end of the summer, to make up for their earlier arguments, and to outdo Alfonso's scooter, Don Cesare bought Totu a brand new Fiat Topolino. My mother's cousins, Tommaso and Santo, home from Rome, took to driving with Totu to the beach at Catanzaro Lido. To distract him, they said. Luigi begged to be brought along with them, but Mother was afraid that the older boys wouldn't watch over him properly. On one excursion, she relented and allowed Luigi to go along with the three young men. I watched enviously as she packed a picnic lunch for the boys, lecturing Luigi not to go swimming unless held by the hand, warning him not to trust the sea water, that it could pull you in the minute you got your feet wet.

"You're going this one time," she told him, "but don't think that you're going with them every week. I know what you're like. You never look before you leap."

Mother shouldn't have worried about Luigi making a habit of the beach, for when he returned in the evening with a sour, sun-burned face and a welt on one cheek, he swore he never wanted to go with such a bunch of show-offs again. He blamed both the sunburn and the bruise on Tommaso, who was known to have a quick temper. First, Luigi recounted, they insisted on stopping for an espresso in the bar at Amato, and stayed there for almost an hour to show off the new car. Then, once at the Lido, they parked the car within sight of the beach but far enough away from it that what Luigi could see of the sea was only a thin, undulating blue-green line. Once the young men changed into their swimming trunks, they asked Luigi to sit on the pavement next to the car to make sure that no one touched it and to wave at them if any *carabinieri* came by. They promised that they would take turns relieving him, but he sat steaming with impatience and heat for what seemed like hours until he couldn't take it any longer and he waved wildly towards the beach. Tommaso, perspiring and as red as the Fiat, came running towards the boy and, seeing no emergency or *carabinieri* in sight, landed a heavy slap on the side of Luigi's sun-sensitized face, leaving his hand-print. Luigi cried and complained that he was hungry and thirsty and needed to go to the bathroom so badly that his stomach hurt. Tommaso dragged him to the beach, pushed him into the ocean, shouting at him to pee as much as he wanted, and called him a *cretino* for tricking him like that, when he could have pissed anywhere along the bushes that bordered the parking spot. If it weren't for Totu, who jumped into the water to help him, Luigi said, Tommaso would have left him alone to sink. Mother was livid at her cousin, but seemed almost satisfied that Luigi had had a bad time.

She told him, "What did you expect to find away from your house? Don't you know that things always sound better than they really are?"

Alfonso knew that even after his sister received the visa papers from Rome, she and Totu were seeing each other again on the sly. He upped the ante and made another revelation that would hurt not only Totu, but his family's reputation and Don Cesare's interests as well.

Everyone in the village simply took it for granted

that Aurora's mother, Paola, slept with her employer, Don Cesare. And who could blame him? His wife, Donna Rachele, looked like a rolled ball of yarn, while Paola had the body of a statue. Her husband Micu drank himself into a stupor whenever he wasn't working.

From the very beginning of his married life, Micu had been made to feel as if he had horns on his head – the cuckolding type of horns the villagers liked to make fun of, so long as no one in their families carried them. Paola may have been a peasant like himself, but she spoke and carried herself like a city woman compared to the costumed village housewives. Micu had responded to the gossip with a shrug. "I don't believe any of it," he told his friends at the bar. "I'm with Don Cesare all the time. All he cares about is his land and olives."

But Micu was blinded by rage when rumours spread that his daughter Aurora had tried to kill herself because Don Cesare's nephew, Totu, had seduced her. He had raised his daughter like a lady, never expecting her to work on the farm, but she still ended up like spoiled goods, taken advantage of by his boss's nephew. And when Totu fled to Rome, Micu would have shot the pampered little "lord" on the spot – had he found him.

Micu's anger, however, had been appeased by his wife and daughter, who had pleaded with him for days not to do anything crazy. After the family's honour was salvaged by Aurora's marriage, Micu returned to spending long nights at the cantina. Paola had expelled him from her bed years before.

Alfonso was his frequent companion there, especially after he negotiated his sister's marriage to Pasquale. Micu and the other men followed the goings-on between Lucia and Totu like a soap opera.

After his sister's engagement, Alfonso's head was full of ideas about his future business dealings in America, where there was real wealth to be made. Alfonso had the land, the olives, and the olive press, but no one to make it all work for him, so he spent hours pumping Micu's head too. He needed his arms and experience in oil-making. Why should Micu keep on caring about Don Cesare's arid orchards when he was treated like a gopher for Don Cesare's right-hand man, the *l'Amatise?*

Alfonso rode his Vespa around the province like a madman, looking for deals for home-made salami and goat cheese, and had Don Cesare laughing when he started working on getting an olive press to compete with him. Alfonso was wasting his money, Don Cesare told everyone. The young man simply didn't have the experience, and most importantly he lacked the contacts needed for selling the oil.

One night at the cantina with Micu, Alfonso came up with a different twist to the stories that had circulated in the village about Paola and Don Cesare. While working in the farmhouse, he had observed the goings-on at Don Cesare's *casale* not far from there, and he agreed with Micu that all the gossip about Don Cesare and his wife was false. It wasn't Don Cesare at all who met his wife there. Alfonso had watched for months on the days when Micu was sent left and right to pick up materials and deliver oil or wheels of crushed olives. On a day when Micu was dispatched to deliver an order in Catanzaro, Alfonso convinced him to follow him to the farm instead.

They hid behind a tree and watched as Gennaro, the *l'Amatise* – Don Cesare's devoted brother-in-law, Totu's father, the serious quiet widower who was too busy to get re-married – paid Paola a visit. The two men waited patiently all afternoon and even saw Gennaro sit on the porch, shirtless, sipping an espresso, and then patted Paola on the behind as she came out to shake a tablecloth. Micu couldn't contain his anger at that sight, but Alfonso forced him to stay quiet. With Micu fuming, they sat behind that tree till late in the afternoon when Gennaro, his shirt back on, left the farmhouse. No wonder Gennaro had interceded for Paola and her children with Don Cesare. Whose children were they?

Micu was ready to get his hunting rifle again, but Alfonso talked sense into him.

The best way to get even with Gennaro and Don Cesare, Alfonso convinced Micu, was to leave them eating dust, leave them to do their own dirty work. Let

Gennaro look for another lackey and someone else's wife. Alfonso promised Micu a share of the profits in the new company if he left Don Cesare's employment and went to live in the farmhouse by the river. There, he would have the power to cut Don Cesare off from the flow of water – and Gennaro from his wife's favours.

Alfonso made sure that the trysts between Paola and Gennaro were made public. The implications went beyond Paola and Gennaro. Totu's past shady encounters with Aurora, which Alfonso swore were real, smelled of incest, as she was probably his half-sister.

After this last revelation, Totu didn't fight back. He became despondent. He cursed his uncle and father and the village and vowed to get out of Mulirena and never set foot there again. To spite Alfonso even more, his friends convinced him that there was still one last card left for him to play. Together they concocted a foolproof, old-fashioned course of action that would keep the couple together and derail Alfonso's plans to become an American millionaire.

Things were moving fast by the end of that summer. Totu walked straight past Piazza Don Carlo on his way to the bar, but he still slipped candies into my hands in exchange for delivering letters to her. Then he sped up and down Via Roma on his Topolino like a crazed mouse. Alfonso's Vespa scooter provided the only motorized competition to the Fiat, but the scooter had an advantage over the car — its ability to race through the narrow alleys and uphill cobblestone streets that led to Piazza Don Carlo and to Lucia's window, now out of bounds to the revved-up Fiat and to Totu.

Peppino's bar had also brought in the first ice-cream maker. Until then, for a summer treat, we kids had had to settle for sucking on an ice cube, unless we walked to Amato for a gelato. In the evenings, instead of going to the Funtanella for water, the young people had taken to going for a *passeggiata* and a gelato in the piazza. We girls changed into our best clothes and walked up and down Via Roma arm-in-arm, acknowledging the other girls with a "*Ciao*," but ignoring the boys.

Since Tina had left for Canada, Lucia had no one to go out with, so she expected me to accompany her on her evening walks. She held me by the hand as if she were taking me for a walk until my friends Rosetta and Bettina joined us. Then the four of us would buy our ice cream and accompany Lucia back to Piazza Don Carlo.

The women who sat on their doorsteps frowned at Lucia, an engaged woman now, for parading herself up and down like that, and criticized her family for permitting it. "If Lucia's in-laws lived in the village," they said, "Rosaria wouldn't be so lax." The woman was too easy-going and too busy caring for her sick husband to notice that Lucia was taking liberties. The only family member who still had control over Lucia's movements was Alfonso, but, in the evenings, he was usually away in the nearby villages, riding his scooter.

Some of the older women even objected to un-married girls parading up and down the piazza, but *nonno* Luigi, rather than disapproving of us, had actu-ally entertained us one evening. He bought each of us lemon-flavoured *granite* and a glass of wine for himself and spoke of his own days in America.

"You're lucky to be going to Montreal," he repeat-ed more than once. "New York is a hell of a place."

My evening *passeggiate* with Lucia ended after the feast of Santo Francesco, which was celebrated in Am-ato in the middle of August. On the Sunday evening of the feast, our piazza was quiet, since most of the younger people had gone to the celebrations. Surpris-ingly, Lucia didn't seem interested in going. After our usual ritual of walking to the piazza, Lucia decided to pick up our water jugs and go to the Funtanella for water. We filled the ceramic water jugs and then, in-stead of walking back to the village, she insisted we walk toward the Timpa. There, we sat on a stone for a long time. It was as though she were waiting for some-one. It irritated me that Lucia didn't talk to me. Since her engagement, she had become closed in with her own thoughts, and acted as if I weren't even there.

The sky turned to dusk, and the cypresses of the cemetery at Amato were discernible only as tall shad-ows against the twilight. I felt uneasy there. I was never comfortable walking by the Timpa, even in daylight. The sheer size of the scooped-out mount, with its exposed rocks jutting out all around, made me feel small and helpless. I asked Lucia to take me back home before it got too dark, saying that Mother would be alarmed by our absence.

Before she responded, we heard a car's engine, and Lucia straightened up. The car sped past us, then doubled back and parked on the side of the road, the engine still running. Two of Totu's friends stayed in the car, while Totu walked towards us and took Lucia by the arm. She turned to me and speaking quickly in a whisper, told me, "I have to go with Totu, so sit here and wait a while before making your way back home, then walk slowly and try not to go home before an hour. And if anyone asks about me say that we went for water together and then on our way back we met some people and we spoke for a while and then I decided to go with them to the feast, and if they ask you who these people are, tell them you don't know them." Lucia spoke so quickly, I hardly understood what she was telling me, except that I would have to walk home alone in the dark. All I could say was, "What about your jug? Won't they think it's stupid for you to be going to the feast with a jug of water?"

"Don't worry about the jug. I'll leave it here and get it back tomorrow morning."

I called back, "Tomorrow? You're only coming back tomorrow morning?"

Totu tried to reassure me. "We're not sure when we'll be back. Caterina, just go home and say that you left Lucia at the Funtanella talking with some people from Amato and you don't know where she is." He squeezed me on the shoulder, and then touched me gently on the cheek, affectionately, as if he understood my fears. "Maybe we'll drive her home first."

Lucia pleaded, "Alfonso can pop up any time. We need at least a couple of hours before they look for us. Caterina is not a baby. She knows her way home.

Totu and Lucia got in the car and drove away, but the car seemed to stop after only a couple of minutes, probably near the cemetery. Alone in the semi-darkness, I sat on a jutting rock and prayed that maybe they would change their minds and return. I waited as I had been instructed and listened for any movement, but all I heard was the sound of crickets coming from the ravine. After what seemed like an eternity, when they had not returned, I started walking slowly towards the village, going over in my head all that Lucia had told me. I was almost halfway to the piazza when I realized that I had also left my own water jug behind. I couldn't go home without it and tell the story I was supposed to tell. Crying in frustration, I started running fast towards the Timpa. I could hear the first explosions of fireworks from Amato and I cried because there I was, all alone in the dark, far from my house, because of Lucia, while other people were having fun at the feast. Then the jerky vroom-vroom sound of a scooter coming from Amato drowned out all other noises, and, as it neared me, it filled the air with what seemed a crescendo of doom. I wanted to hide, but Alfonso rode by me almost instantly and then stopped. I was shaking with fear.

"Where are you going at this time, alone?" he asked.

I told him I had gone for water and forgotten my jug at the Timpa.

"Didn't Lucia come with you? Where did she go?"

Before I had time to finish saying what Lucia had told me to say, Alfonso scooped me up, sat me behind the scooter and, in a flash, dropped me at the Timpa. He spotted Lucia's jug next to mine and, cursing San Francesco and other saints, got back on the scooter, turned his head towards me and yelled, "Wait for me. I know where they're hiding. I saw the jerk's car parked on the road."

I crunched against the side of the mount and, to ease my fright, I closed my eyes and wished I was dreaming. Within a few minutes the scooter again broke the silence. I opened my eyes as a crying Lucia fell on the ground in front of me.

"I'm not coming home," Lucia screamed as she got up. "I'm running away from this stinking village."

Alfonso jumped from the scooter, towards us, as if to strike Lucia. Instead, he took my water jug and hit it against a stone, smashing it to pieces. The cold spring water splashing on my legs made me jump.

"This is your last *passeggiata* to the Funtanella – you have to forget this place once and for all." He grabbed Lucia by the arm and looked directly in her eyes as he spoke, "You're going to America and you're never going to drink this water again. Do you understand? You're going to America, whether in one piece or not. You won't say a word about this to anyone, or I'll smash your head like this." He released her, pitched the second water jug against the rocks, then took Lucia by the hair and hurled her back on the ground. As he jumped back onto his scooter, he kept on talking. "If the *signurinu l'Amatise* had any balls, he would have come out of his hiding place. He can't be far away. I'm going to find him and smash his face to the ground where he belongs." Then, before taking off, he leaned his face down toward me and said slowly and firmly, "Caterinè, don't say a word to anyone about this. Make sure the *puttana* gets back home."

I felt as shattered as my broken jug, which my grandfather had bought for me at the fair years before. I picked up a couple of shards, as if trying to put the jug back together again. Then I cried uncontrollably.

"I'll get you a new one," Lucia said, sobbing.

"Don't you know we're both leaving? What will we do with a jug in America?" I wailed.

Lucia kept on sobbing and made no move to walk back home.

"Aren't we going home?" I pleaded.

"You go. I'll wait a few more minutes. Maybe Totu will change his mind and come back for me."

I was too scared to walk alone. "I'll wait with you," I said. I felt guilty, as if this were all my fault. Had I not forgotten my jug, I might have made it back to the village on time without being seen, and Lucia and Totu could have eloped.

"What happened to Totu?" I asked. "I don't understand anything," she said. "Everything happened so fast. He left."

The last outbursts of fireworks at Amato filled the skies with a machine-gun succession of shots, and then complete stillness followed. It was only when the first chattering of people walking back home to Mulirena could be heard across the ravine that Lucia got up. "Let's go before everyone sees us like this. He won't be coming any more," she mumbled, and we set off for home, both sobbing.

Half way home, Alfonso came back for us, motioned to his sister to get on the back seat of the scooter. She sat me on her lap. Before setting off, Alfonso yelled, "What a good-for-nothing coward! And you wanted to run away with him?"

When I arrived home without my jug, I had to tell my worried Mother what had happened. She was upset, but mostly at Lucia. "How can she be so *fessa?* Doesn't she know by now that he's been taking her for a ride? Totu will never marry her, or he'd have done something by now. I hope to God she changes her head in the next couple of months, or she'll be left with nothing."

The day after, Mother talked about Totu only with Giovanna, and in whispered tones, even though no one else was at the shop. The story Giovanna heard was that, while Mulirena was deserted because of the celebrations in Amato, Totu and Lucia were supposed to spend some time alone at the farm hut that belonged to Totu's family, on the outskirts of Amato, next to the cemetery. His two friends were to keep Alfonso occupied and drunk at the *osteria,* so he wouldn't realize his sister was not home till late into the night. By that time, after all the revelers in Amato had also gone home, Totu was to drive Lucia to his friend's home in Amato and spend the night. In the morning the couple and two witnesses would present themselves to the municipal office and ask to be married in a civil ceremony, after which neither side of the family could do anything to stop them from being together again. Even if the civil marriage did not go through, the two had spent the night together and were as good as married in everyone's eyes. Alfonso would have to deal with Pasquale's brothers, who would certainly reclaim the scooter and whatever money Pasquale had paid for. Lucia's honour would be saved by marriage.

No one knew exactly how or why Totu disappeared in the night. Alfonso never said anything to anyone for fear that his sister's future in-laws would hear about it. Lucia shut herself up in her house and didn't talk to anyone. Totu didn't give anyone an explanation either, as he took the first train to Rome without saying goodbye to any of his friends.

"I still don't understand what kind of fish he is," Mother said to Giovanna.

After that night, Lucia stopped coming out in the evening with me. She became more quiet and glum, even as she prepared a new wardrobe.

Part IV

The deceptions and subterfuges that women were forced to use in those villages of Calabria! If the morals of the women there were above reproach, why was there so much gossip about illicit affairs, love triangles, cuckolded husbands, and out-of-wedlock births? Even though the price paid by pregnant, unmarried girls was most often to leave the village and go work as maids in the cities, such cases were known to happen. The men bragged all the time about their love conquests, so with whom did they have these amorous adventures? Women were criticized for so much as speaking to a man who was not a close friend or relative. Something didn't line up. I could not believe that the intelligent, spirited women I knew suffered this repression in silence without questioning it.

"Why did you put up with it?" I'd like to confront my mother.

I know her answer already; I've heard it many times before. "The world is made like that. It's the way things were, there, at the time."

My mother never looked back at the village with rose-tinted glasses, and she never suffered from nostalgia for what she left behind. When we landed in Halifax, she made the sign of the cross and told herself she would never make the crossing again. Yet, she, like other women of her generation, brought the village with them. In the early years, she held on to its medieval mores with a tenacity that brought me to tears over and over again as a teenager in Montreal.

"You can only straighten a tree when it's very young," she told me after one of our many arguments.

She mellowed with the years, once she was assured that her young shoot had developed strong roots. But the inconsistency of her both shunning the malice of village politics and yielding to the tyranny of its demands used to exasperate me.

"Whatever is destined, will happen. You can't fight destiny," she often said. That resignation also drove me wild.

I still cannot quite understand what to make of the concept of destiny. It's like a mystery of faith: one believes it without needing to understand it. Do Italians make more of it than other people? My father referred to it as *la forza del destino,* the force of destiny, after his favourite Verdi opera. I can't decide whether the women's blind belief in destiny is what gave them their courage and quiet strength, or whether it was the cop-out that kept them submissive to the harsh demands imposed on them.

"You still worry about what people say," I'd shout, when my mother forbade me to do what other girls my age did.

"And you only think about yourself," she'd holler back.

The constant tug-of-war with my mother eventually created a wall between us that made it hard to discuss matters of the heart and especially of the body. I'll never know what destiny really meant for her as a woman, though her great generosity of spirit towards family comes quickly to mind, and perhaps family was what made her invoke destiny as often as she did.

As I look back at the events that led to Lucia's engagement, I remember the comments I heard spoken gravely and in acquiescence at the seamstress's shop. "She has three brothers to think about," a heavy responsibility for a sixteen-year-old girl, torn not only by family feuds, but also by the expectation that she should be a help to her family.

Lucia married by proxy at the end of August. I wore my white, first communion dress as I walked behind her holding her long, white veil. Lucia could have chosen to go through a civil ceremony at the town hall and celebrate the religious wedding in Montreal, as many other proxy brides had done, but she insisted on carrying out the full event in Mulirena. "I know no one in Montreal," she said. "It had been promised that I would marry here, and I'm marrying here."

She planned the whole event as though Pasquale were present. He paid for it all – the food, drinks, her dress, shoes, and flowers. She wanted to have the best wedding that Mulirena had ever seen. Giovanna sewed a slim white satin gown and spent hours covering by hand the tiny buttons that went all the way from her neckline down to below her waist. She had copied the dress from the wedding picture of the Duchess of Wales in a magazine. Lucia carried a bouquet of orange blossoms and had the longest veil I had ever seen.

When Lucia tried the dress on a week before the wedding, at her house, I saw her cry. She held her tears as long as her mother was in the room, but when Comare Rosaria left, Lucia broke down, and I didn't know what to say, as I held the long veil off the floor.

"I have no other choice," she said, sobbing, after she wiped her eyes with the hem of her white dress. "I'll pretend to be happy for my family. That's all we women are expected to do – pretend we're happy and live for our families." I never saw her cry again.

Comare Rosaria worked all week baking cookies and frying three types of *braciole*, croquettes made with meat, potato and rice. Pasquale's family arrived a day earlier than planned and took over the whole house.

"Poor Comare Rosaria," Mother said. "She has to shoulder all that work by herself." The woman had to cook for and accommodate over a dozen people while getting everything ready for the wedding feast, with little help from the rest of the family.

The morning of the wedding, the house was filled with guests, who were served coffee, *biscotti*, Vermouth, Anice, Strega, and *Mille Fiori*. The bride's father couldn't walk all the way to the church, so Lucia was accompanied by Alfonso. They were followed, procession-like, by the best man, the groom's older brother, and his wife, by Comare Rosaria and her younger son, by Pasquale's parents and other members of his family, and all the other guests. Mother and the older women wore their own wedding costumes, with the long skirt, bodice and ribbons of pastel-coloured satin, with their white *mancale*. It was one of the few occasions they had to wear it. It would be the last time Mother ever wore hers.

As the procession advanced slowly towards the church, from their balconies people threw rice at the bride – a symbol of good luck, prosperity and fertility. Family members threw confetti. Children ran along the side of the road, trying to catch as many of the white candy-coated almonds as possible. As the bride approached the church, the altar boys pulled the ropes of the church bells with all of their strength, making them ring incessantly and joyfully.

Don Raffaele celebrated the Mass and blessed the bride. Her brother, Alfonso, and new brother-in-law, Matteo, signed the register as witnesses. Lucia's veil was raised from her face and she walked out the church with Matteo, who stood in for Pasquale.

At the reception, guests were served the croquettes, trays of *amaretti,* and glasses of sparkling wine with slices of a white wedding cake. The guests received a *bomboniera,* a pretty porcelain bowl that held more confetti, wrapped in white tulle.

"Comare Rosaria prepared a beautiful feast," Mother told *U Grancu* the following day from our balcony. "Nothing was spared."

"Except for a plate of pasta and a groom in the bed," *U Grancu* spurted out.

"Be quiet," Mother said, afraid that Comare Rosaria would hear. "They'll have time, soon enough, for both."

Later, she said, "Some men can only think of two things, their stomachs and bed."

"Don Cesare made a big mistake when he sent Totu to Rome the first time," was Giovanna's verdict about the sad ending of Lucia's love story with Totu. "Maybe it would have all turned differently if Totu had never gone to Rome. Rome ruined many men."

I still couldn't understand what must have gone

through Totu's head. I had seen him look up Lucia's balcony with wistful eyes, cry like a puppy when she received her visa papers, and drive away with her on the last night of their encounter. According to the women at Giovanna's shop, he was as much to blame for the turn of events as Alfonso and Don Cesare.

I first saw Rome as a child when father had to get his visa. The city overwhelmed me with its grandeur. What must it have been like for Totu and the young men of Mulirena who went to Rome for the first time, hardly out of boyhood? What was it about Rome that made the three men dispose of their childhood sweethearts so easily? On my second visit to Rome, accompanied by my mother's brother, Zio Pietro, we spent time alone with Totu and he finally confessed, sort of.

The city came on to me loud, brash, and in constant motion. After a bumpy six-hour ride on the train, my first sight of the city outside Stazione Termini overcame me with a sense of confusion close to vertigo. The year before we had come to Rome with Father for his visa, and the noise of the traffic had given both Mother and me a headache. This time it seemed that there were even more cars and motor scooters speeding by, honking their loud horns in a cacophony of city noise unlike anything heard in the village, where the occasional herd of sheep, one car, one small truck, and one motor scooter would upset the quiet.

My mother's cousin Tommaso picked us up and walked us to the palazzo on Via Merulana where he lived with his brother Santo and Michele. Totu had lived with them the first time he went to Rome, but this time, Tommaso said, he had gone to live with a friend from university. Tommaso took me by the hand, but even with him there, we had to wait forever to cross the wide piazzas; the drivers rarely relented to pedestrians. I was paralyzed by fear. How would I ever be able to cross the streets if I were alone?

Zio Pietro asked Tommaso about Totu. Had he seen him?

"Yes. He'll come by to see you later, but don't talk about Lucia. He's a bit confused, but he did well to return here," Tommaso said. "Once you live in Rome, you can't live in the village anymore. Just ask Michele and Santo if they want to come back."

The two young tailors were in Rome because of Tommaso, who had come a few years before, having heard that good tailors were in high demand. Most men from Mulirena went to Milan, where they found jobs as stonemasons, carpenters, or just plain labourers. To save money, the men lived together in makeshift quarters on the periphery of the city and returned home only for holidays. Because of the exorbitant cost of decent housing, few could hope to bring their families there, which is how it became a commonly acceptable way of life for married couples to live apart for years, and to see each other only at Christmas, Easter and the summer holidays.

Because of the roughness of their work, and because of their speech and peasant manners, southerners were nicknamed *terroni* – of the earth – by the northerners in Milan. Most of these southerners dreamed only of making enough money to feed and clothe their families and to buy a new suit for themselves with which to impress the *paesani* on their visits to the village.

Those who went to Rome were of a different class. They were skilled artisans, mostly tailors. Their long apprenticeships in tailor shops and their years of painstaking needlework served them well in a city that favoured custom tailoring. Tommaso found a job and a place to stay near the train station and had a following of loyal clients who appreciated his meticulous workmanship, not only for men's suits, but for ladies' *tailleurs* as well. Tailored ladies' suits were very popular at the time and coordinated well with the short *alla maschietta* haircuts of the fashionable Romane.

Tommaso had spoken of his good fortune in Rome to his friends during his visits to Mulirena. After only a few months of working there, he befriended a fifty-year-old widow. She offered Tommaso a room in her large apartment, and he accepted on condition that he could bring his brother and set up his own shop there.

The apartment on the second floor of the palazzo faced Santa Maria Maggiore. Tommaso had described the place in so much detail that, when we arrived the first time, it was as though I had already lived there. It was reached by an open elevator with wrought-iron doors; it had a large foyer with gilt mirrors, a hanging chandelier, and a dining room with heavy, ornate furniture. A small kitchen, a bathroom, and four bedrooms opened off a dark corridor. Tommaso behaved as if the apartment on Via Merulana belonged to him, and wouldn't dream of going back to live in Mulirena.

The widow who owned the apartment and her twenty-year-old daughter Loredana joined us for dinner. It was Loredana, Tommaso told us, who introduced the group of young men to her circle of friends. She had also helped Totu find his way around the university's bureaucracy the first time he was sent to Rome by his uncle. I imagined and envied the young men and Loredana's friends going out in groups, taking rides on motor scooters, going to the cinema and the beach in Ostia. No wonder, I thought, the men took to the new Roman life so quickly. I also felt a tinge of resentment. While the young men lived in the carefree world of the movie *Le Ragazze di Piazza di Spagna* that I had daydreamed about, the girls of Piazza d'Amore had been jilted and left behind to their silent tears, destined to a life of duty and unfulfilled yearnings.

"In the *paese*, you can only talk to girls in sign

language," Michele told us, to justify himself for breaking his engagement to Tina. "You get a chance to touch a woman only after you marry. And what if there's nothing worth touching?"

To lie on a beach in Ostia, next to a semi-nude Roman girl, and to be caressed by one, must have been a heady experience for Michele. He said he felt that the most honourable thing to do was to leave Tina as soon as possible. Other men with similar experiences chose to keep and marry their village girlfriends, while continuing to enjoy the favours of the more liberated city women.

He added, "Here you can breathe. Rome is something else!"

"And the women!" Tommaso said, winking at Michele. "Ask Michele about the women, and the conquests he's made already."

Michele grinned in response. He looked slimmer and wore his hair differently than in the village – a long chunk of wavy hair falling on his eyes. He looked like a movie star.

"I want a future in Rome," he said, "like Tommaso."

"Eh," Tommaso added. "Rome will always be Rome!"

Just then Totu appeared, unannounced, and chimed in, "Rome was, is, and probably always will be a city built as a monument to the egos of conquerors.

But Michele and I are thinking of different conquests, eh Michele?" Then he sheepishly shook hands and kissed all of us. "Welcome to Rome," he said while pinching me on the cheek.

Tommaso and Zio Pietro convinced Mother to prolong our stay by a couple of days, after spending the entire next day at the Canadian Embassy to get our visa.

"When will you and the kids get the chance to see Rome again?" Zio said.

The next day, Totu took us to explore Rome. As we walked past grey stone buildings, fountains, and statues built to the scale of giants and gods, I understood Rome's reputation for things colossal and eternal. I could not help but feel my own smallness. I felt a real sense of physical fright when I stood in front of the larger-than-life statues in St. Peter's Basilica.

Totu made us observe how each epoch had left its landmark structure on the city: the arc of Augustus, the Coliseum, Castel Santangelo, St. Peter's. When we stood in front of the Monument to the Fatherland in Piazza Venezia, he said to Zio Pietro, "Remember, Mussolini's humiliation – his hanging head down while people spat in his face and kicked his shins – was made into a public spectacle, not in Rome, but in Milan. Is it not significant?"

"He deserved what he got," Zio said, "in Milan or Rome."

"Yes, but the image that has remained of Il Duce

in Rome is that of the young proud leader who stood on that balcony in 1922 and called to his countrymen to follow him." We all gazed at the all-white marble building, layered like a wedding cake, which overpowers the square with its bulk and was built, Totu said, just in time for Mussolini's March on Rome.

"Just think, Pietro. Twenty-six thousand people gathered in the square to cheer him on that day, and millions of Italians at home and abroad believed they had found the man to return them to the glory of ancient Rome. It's mind-boggling. Now it's the so-called Democrats who are herding in people like sheep."

"Let's not start talking politics here," Zio said. He was a staunch Christian Democrat, and Totu knew it.

But Totu was in a talkative mood. Over *panini* eaten on a park bench at Villa Borghese, the conversation turned to Mulirena, and Totu talked non-stop, as if wanting to unburden himself.

He started by saying that the quarrels he had left behind seemed by now as insignificant as the squabbles between the pigeons in the gardens around us. The first time he ran away, he had felt like a ragged marionnette pulled by the strings of petty village politics, with both his uncle and Lucia badgering him with one angry letter after another. Then he was new to the city and trying to make his way in university.

"That first year was very difficult, and no one in Mulirena understood that," he said. His uncle had wanted him to enter law school, but he barely managed to get admitted to the university in literature. Even at that, he had to struggle to keep up with the other university students, whose language proficiency was far superior to his. At first, he said, he partook in the outings and activities of the group headed by Loredana and Santo, who had become a couple. After his initial curiosity, though, Totu found her and most of her friends insipid and shallow, and he became bored with their company. He joined them only when they went to the cinema. His studies took up much of his free time. For spending money, he had to count on his uncle, who infuriated him with news of provincial politics and expected Totu to make new connections in Rome.

"This is not Catanzaro, where we know everyone and everyone knows us," he said. "My uncle never understood this."

Lucia also insisted on a commitment from him, especially after Michele broke his engagement to her friend, Tina. "She thought I had fallen for a Roman woman."

I remember the note he sent her at the time. "Rome is full of beautiful and available women, but my mind and heart are taken up by other interests and concerns that you cannot understand. I want to end the story with you and all of Mulirena."

Ending his relationship with Lucia that first time,

he explained, was the first step out of the inertia he wanted badly to escape. In time he connected with a group of Political Science students and started attending discussion meetings with them. A nucleus formed. They met regularly after classes and late into the night. Totu experienced a sense of belonging with this community of intellectuals that he had never felt before. They read and studied the writings of Antonio Gramsci. He tried to explain to Zio about Gramsci's ideals of creating an alliance between the peasants of the south and the workers of the north. As a student, he said, his role was clearly identified by Gramsci: "An elite of 'organic intellectuals' who would bring about a new social order in post-Fascist Italy." He spoke with passion. "In the south, you have all become puppets of Rome and care little about the proletariat."

My uncle got up to stretch his legs, wanting to change the conversation. I knew Mother was itching to ask him about the events of his last night in Mulirena.

After a long pause, she asked him, "Totu, let's talk seriously now. If you wanted to end it with Lucia, why didn't you leave her alone then? Why did you use this child for your own dirty tricks?"

I wanted to disappear behind the bushes.

"Teresa, you're right," he sounded contrite. "It was a barbaric way of doing things, what we tried to do. That's why I couldn't go through with it. We're not living in the Middle Ages, but nothing happened between us." Then he turned to me. "I apologize, Caterina, for that evening."

I didn't know what to answer, and only shrugged as if to say, "It's OK."

He continued, "I feel I owe you an explanation, but this remains between us. Everyone thinks I ran away because I was afraid of Alfonso. The truth is, I couldn't go ahead with the farce my friends had set up for me, out of principle. It's hard to explain. In Mulirena I become a different person, one I don't like. That's why I had to get away. I'll never set foot there again."

"Eh, don't be foolish," Zio answered. "You still have your father there. Of course you're going back."

"My father is dead to me, after last summer, but, Teresa, I have to admit, I love Lucia and always will. My intentions were honourable, but the means were not. I could only make a clean break with Mulirena by ending my relationship with Lucia. The Party has now become my religion and my only love."

On the train back, Zio and Mother spoke again about Totu. "He's confused and full of shit. He cares more about his ideas than real people," Zio said.

"He grew up without a mother, and his father was never there for him," Mother said. "Still, I don't understand him. He's so intelligent that sometimes he doesn't make any sense to me."

I didn't understand all that Totu had tried to say either, though I understood why Lucia liked being with him so much. Totu was different from the other men. To feel that he had arrived, Tommaso found room at the palazzo. Michele set out to conquer as many Roman girls as possible. Totu had higher goals. He wanted to own the city. From the anxiety in his voice, I sensed the same paralyzing fear of Rome I felt, which he could only conquer by cutting all ties to Mulirena. Lucia was the helpless casualty of the battle.

Once we had our visas, our departure suddenly became real. I looked on at every village activity as the last of its kind. Mulirena's carnival period started in early February, when families took turns slaughtering their pigs and helping each other with the messy job of cutting the meat and making provisions for the year. Mother, Luigi, and I spent an evening at Nanna Caterina's house, making sausages. The women sat around the table with a metal sausage maker clamped to its edge. One woman fed the cut-up meat into the machine's top opening, turning the handle that pushed the meat into the pig's intestines. I watched as the long slimy tubes, plumped up with red meat and speckled with white fat, slithered and curved onto the table like snakes. Another woman pricked the sausages with a safety pin to let out the air, while another tied them tightly into links.

All evening, I had wanted to help. Nanna let me do some pricking, but I wanted to go through the whole process by myself. When they finished, late at night, Nanna gave me some scrap meat and some intestine to play with – just when Mother was ready to go home.

"Let her stay; she can sleep here," Nanna Caterina said. "You're going away in two weeks. Who knows if I'll ever see her again."

Mother wasn't convinced. Since the incident at the Timpa with Lucia, I had become fearful and clingy, especially late at night, but I wanted to stay. While Nanna cleaned up and got ready for bed, I played at turning the handle and stuffing and tying the tube, as I had seen the others do, though I was disappointed that my sausage turned out skinny and soft.

After Nanna had finished washing the pans and cleaning the table, she undressed and asked me if I needed to go to the bathroom. The cold, smelly cubicle was in a dark corner of the house, so I said I didn't need to go. I went to bed with my clothes on, since it was quite cold, next to her. She slept in the middle between me and Nannu Luigi.

I had often slept with my other Nanna, but never here. After the lights were turned off, the room looked completely different and foreign. I couldn't fall asleep. When I slept as a baby at Nanna Stella, she used to sing me a lullaby about wolves eating a sheep, and now the shadows all looked like wolf faces. If I closed my eyes, I saw myself alone at the Timpa, terrified by the darkness. If I opened my eyes, I was just as scared by the shadows made by the moonlight shining on the white-washed walls through the slits in the closed window.

I regretted having stayed over just to make a flabby sausage. Grandfather snored and made all kinds of strange noises, I was afraid to move and fall off the side of the narrow bed, and I felt uncomfortable sleeping with my clothes on. I started to cry, softly at first, and then, more loudly. Nanna heard the sobbing and asked me if I wanted some water, or maybe I needed to go to the washroom? Crying so much, I gasped for air, I said I wanted to go to my own home to sleep.

"At this hour? It's past midnight," Nanna said.

"Take her home, *ppe la Madonna*," Nannu shouted. "Or no one is getting any sleep here tonight."

The old woman got out of bed, dressed me up in my coat, and then put on her own outer winter clothes with a heavy, black *mancale* over her head. We went out into the cold February night. The deserted streets were lit by a sky full of sharp, bright stars and a smiling crescent moon, and I felt happy again – except for Nanna grumbling all the way up the hill. She said she could hardly feel her hands and legs anymore. She had been up since dawn, chopping the gristly meat for *capicolli* and sausages, salting the *prosciutti*, pickling the hog's head for *ialatina*, boiling and stirring its blood for blood pudding. She couldn't count how many times she had rinsed out the greasy pots and pans with frigid water. And now, to complete her day, she really needed this *passeggiata* at this ungodly hour, with the *signorina* from Piazza Don Carlo!

When we got home, Mother answered the knock on the door, wearing her long white shirt and holding a lantern in her hand. She looked fearful that something had happened. *Nanna* Caterina just pushed me inside the house, happy to be rid of me. She said crossly, "Here, here, you can have her."

Mother sounded very angry with me in front of her mother-in-law. She exclaimed, "*Oi!* Something told me this would happen. What could we expect? Go to bed with children, wake up with fleas."

At this point, I started crying again, imagining I would get a good spanking from my mother for my acting so childishly. Instead, when Nanna left, Mother tucked me into the warm bed next to her, kissed me, and whispered gently, "Stop crying now. It's nothing serious, as long as nothing's happened to you, and you're safe at home."

Part V

I sit in contemplation in my bedroom, trying to ward off sleep. I've been shut in for three days, transposed to another time, in an almost different dimension. What is the relationship between that ten-year-old girl and the woman sitting alone on a bed cluttered with notebooks, wanting to write the quintessential Calabrian love story?

The people I've revisited are not only old friends and neighbours; they formed the life I was born into. With my eyes half-closed, I see them all appearing like still frames on an old grainy movie reel. I have lived in the shadows of these characters without ever realizing it. To what extent have they dictated how I've lived my own life till now?

I'm reliving the stories from a different place and time, and I can't help but question motives and actions that at the time went ignored or simply untold. If Aurora had been really pregnant when she tried to commit suicide, and Totu was not the father, who was? No one spoke of the missing piece to that puzzle. Aurora, a girl named after the dawn, was callously nicknamed a "little gypsy" in the same way that real gypsies were spoken about – people of no account, without homes, whose lives were not worth talking about.

This story has no proper ending yet, its characters suspended, as if in transit, in the labyrinth of my imagination. I know that stories need a beginning, a middle, and an end. How – or when – do you give a story floating in space its final resolution?

"Invent, invent," is the writing instructor's mantra. Is this what writers do when truth escapes them? Already, in looking back to my childhood years, I can hardly determine if what I remember are dreams or facts. What I'm certain about is that I and the village women I've known all carry a history and worlds of stories within us – all worth telling. I'll need to set my reminiscences on paper, not only to preserve the memories but to find a compass for my own peregrinations. It's a well-worn truism: How can I know where I'm going, if I don't understand where I've come from?

For now, I relish having relived the delight and joy I derived from those evening *passeggiate* with the girls. There's one other special person who comes into my thoughts only now and then, but whenever he does, he also makes me smile.

In Mulirena, school was dismissed at lunch every day. Signor Gavano used to engage me in a little guessing game as we walked home.

"Signora Maria is having *minestra* today," he'd say. "But it smells different from usual. What do you think it is, Caterina?"

I would take a whiff and answer: "I think it's the zucchini flowers."

"Signora Paola is frying *pipe e patate*... again. Didn't she have that yesterday?" I liked the way he pronounced the dialect expressions.

Fried peppers and potatoes were a very common meal, and one of the easiest to detect, unless the fishmonger had been in the village. Then, from every other household, there emanated the sizzle and odour of tiny smelts frying in olive oil, and I would nod and laugh each time he repeated *pisci friuti*.

As we reached Piazza Don Carlo, he'd ask: "Now guess, Caterina. If yesterday I had *pasta e faggioli*; Tuesday, *pasta e fave*; Monday, *pasta e rape*; what do you think I'll be having today?"

"*Pasta e patate?*" I might have ventured with a smile. Donna Rachele, his landlady and cook, had a very limited and predictable repertoire.

"Ah, maybe, but... it could also be *pasta e broccoli*. I'll tell you tomorrow, but whatever it is, it will be delicious," he'd say with a wink and a little squeeze on my shoulder. I'd turn toward my house and he'd walk up one house further to where Don Cesare and Donna Rachele lived.

I remember Signor Gavano in tones of tan and sand. It must have been because he wore a tweedy jacket with little brown and beige squares. His hair was tawny blonde: fine and straight and parted to one side. His pants and shirts were always impeccably clean and well pressed, and he spoke the most limpid Italian I had ever heard.

I don't remember my first-grade teacher well, except that she was pregnant and was replaced by a teacher from Catanzaro in the middle of the year. This new teacher was big-breasted and had the haughty posture of all the *signore* from the city. She was always hot and tired. She would sit by her desk, which was on an elevated platform, and fan herself, complaining about the flies, while the class ran around in circles. When an inspector from the city school headquarters was expected to visit, the teacher tutored us for days on how to answer his questions. She instructed us to always look at her hands, which would be crossed behind her back. If the inspector asked a math question, she would stand or bend her waist strategically to give us the right answer. When the inspector asked how we liked our new teacher, I was the only one to confess that I liked the other one better. The Signora taught us second grade too, and the chances were that she would bring us through to fifth grade, as it was the tradition in the schools there for a teacher to take the same group from the first to fifth grades.

One day, this teacher asked the class to study a passage about love of country from the book *Cuore* by Edmondo De Amicis. In the evening, I read it over and over, and by the next day I could recite it by heart. The teacher, impressed, paraded me in front of the third, fourth, and fifth grade classes to show off how well she had taught her student.

Walking into each class, I felt nervous and afraid I would forget everything. But each time I stood on the elevated platform in front of the teacher's desk, I was able to recite, *Perché Amo l'Italia da* Edmondo De Amicis:

> I love Italy because my mother is Italian, because the blood that runs through my veins is Italian, because Italian is the soil in which are buried the dead for whom my mother weeps, and whom my father venerates. Because the city where I was born, the language that I speak, the books that I read, because my brother, my sister, my friends, and the people that I live with, and the beautiful nature that surrounds me, and all that I see, that I love, that I study, that I admire is Italian. Because.... because...

From that day on the Signora gave me preferential treatment. Most days, she would bring her torn and flimsy sheets, her husband's worn-out socks and undershirts, and have me sit on the large balcony to do her mending while the other students had to repeat the addition and multiplication tables ad nauseam. I had the company of the housewives who chatted from one balcony to the other and exchanged notes on what they were cooking for lunch.

Signor Gavano came to teach fourth grade at about the same time that my father left for Canada. The new teacher never expressed any scorn about the condition of the schoolhouse or the village, which must have been a world apart from where he came from, and he called all the women, including the peasants, Signore.

From her balcony, Donna Rachele liked to brag to everyone that she never even had to make Signor Gavano's bed or clean his room. He cleaned up after himself, unlike the men in the village. Donna Rachele even whispered to Mother that in the evenings, she often saw him make the sign of the cross and bend his head in prayer before going to bed. In Mulirena, showing religious piety was reserved for women and children.

Besides the history of the village, Signor Gavano taught me how to speed-read a book, by reading the first sentence of a paragraph and scanning the rest.

When Signor Gavano heard I was leaving for

Canada, he joked sadly that soon he wouldn't even have a job in Calabria because the kids were all going away. He taught us about Canada's forests and lakes and its abundance of fresh running water – undoubtedly what he had learned from his old geography books. One day, he showed us a map of Canada, coloured green for forests, with splashes of blue for the lakes and rivers. Then he placed a minuscule boot-shaped piece of paper next to it, to show the difference in size of the two countries. He spoke of *un immensitá di spazii,* and the word "immensity" took on the shape and colour of the silent forests of Canada. There was no mention of cities or people, as though Canada were only land and water.

Signor Gavano went back to his home at the end of fourth grade, but returned in the fall to teach the fifth grade class. By then, the village had embarked on the construction of new public buildings, and the school was moved from a converted house in the centre of the village to a new, separate building, which it shared with the municipal office. It was built on an open field, *il Campo Sportivo*, a sport's field used mostly by boys playing soccer or riding their bicycles. The new classrooms didn't have any balconies, but their large windows faced a wheat field, with stubby fig trees scattered here and there. When the midday sun hit the windowpanes, the whole classroom seemed to sparkle in brilliant sunlight.

I remember the day I went to say goodbye to my fourth grade classmates and to Signor Gavano. It was at the end of January. The wheat field, which in summer had shimmered in flaxen yellow, dotted with red poppies, was now reduced to wet stubbles of straw, and the fig tree branches struggled and bent with the wind and the rain. My friends had little going away gifts for me: embroidered handkerchiefs, doilies, a scarf. Signor Gavano surprised me with the gift of *I Promessi Sposi*, the novel I would have studied in high school had I remained in Italy. He took my hand and held it in his. He looked into my eyes and wished me *un bel avvenire*.

"You're going to a big country," he said. "You'll have many opportunities. But don't forget us. After all, Italy too is a big country."

He had crystal-clear, aquamarine eyes.

I loved him.

We left Mulirena on February 31, 1957, on the same day that the first TV set was brought to the village. I spent the rainy January afternoon with mother, Luigi, and Zio Pietro, shuffling the contents of our bulging suitcases, agonizing over what to bring and what to leave behind, while a constant stream of people came by, bringing more pungent-smelling parcels to add to the pile of what was left to be packed. They came with letters tied to packages of homemade cheeses, salamis, and dried oregano to be delivered to their close friends and relatives in Montreal. Zio grumbled with each last-minute addition, and Luigi and I grew impatient because we wanted to go out and see the TV set that Peppino, the bar owner, had received that morning, and that everyone who came by was talking about.

But then, the butcher's daughter who worked across from the bar told us not to bother, that Peppino had turned the TV off and sent all the gawkers away. She had watched the commotion from her shop that morning. Peppino's sons and the bar regulars had unpacked the set impatiently, taking turns adjusting and tuning it, only to stare at fuzzy snow and jumpy white lines. She finally went over and yelled at them to at least turn off the ear-piercing sound, if they were going to stand there, transfixed like *babbi* for the rest of the day. Peppino explained to her and to the crowd that had gathered around that the sound proved that the TV set was in good working order. He invited everyone to return later when the television would truly come to life. He would serve free espresso and *bibite* while they all watched the one and only program scheduled that evening, *Lascia o Raddoppia,* a game show that all of Italy was raving about. Of course, by then, we would be leaving for Santa Eufemia to catch the ten o'clock train for Naples. I felt like I was leaving a party just when things were beginning to happen.

The start of winter had been milder and had seemed less somber to me than usual. Nanna Stella had

151

wrapped green tomatoes from the summer's bumper crop in newspapers, and they had ripened slowly. It was unheard of, she said, to eat red tomatoes until the end of January. Mother spoke less and less of the war days, when all they'd had to eat were wild field greens and a few thin slices of rationed yellow cornbread. Now the bread was baked at Nanna's store and was white and plentiful. And, for snacks, she spread it with *formaggino,* the triangular-shaped little creamy cheeses wrapped in silver foil.

Since we had received our visa, there wasn't a day that someone didn't offer me something to eat or drink and say, "Eat the *capicollo*" – or the fig, or the chestnuts – "while you can, for you're never going to see them again."

While Mother reminded me of all the good things around us that we would be leaving for good, she also smirked at the desire for luxury that was sweeping the village. *Che lusso!* she'd say, whenever we allowed ourselves a new indulgence.

The Amatesi had not only gotten their ice-cream maker before the Mulerinesi. They had also been able to watch the black-and-white television screen at their local bar almost a full year earlier. Many of the men and boys had walked to Amato every Thursday evening to watch *Lascia o Raddoppia*. In the show, contestants were asked impossibly difficult questions on geography, history, politics, and literature. After a first correct answer, they won a large sum of money. They then had to decide whether to walk away with their winnings – *lascia* – or take a chance with another question and double the loot – *raddoppia* – if they answered correctly. If they were wrong, they lost everything. The show's host was Mike Buongiorno, a suave, good-looking man who had gotten the name Mike after a short stint living in New York. The day after each show, the talk around the village was of how much money had been won or lost. Most of the amounts, in the millions of lire, sounded astronomical and unreal to the villagers. The whole nation was glued to the TV set every Thursday evening, watching the winners, who became millionaires and instant national celebrities.

In Mulirena, part of our newly felt prosperity was due to the dollar bills that my father and other men sent in each letter to their families. This allowed our mothers to buy us *formaggini*, *gelati*, and new clothes.

But now, after almost two years of living apart, our family would finally be together. And Lucia would be travelling with us to join the husband she had never met. We would be boarding the boat, *Saturnia*, in Naples on the last day of February. We would arrive in Halifax eleven days later. Mother could not speak of the voyage without her eyes widening with panic. She had never ventured beyond Mulirena unaccompanied. And now she would have to cross an ocean, in the depths of winter, alone with two children and the ever-willful Lucia. Since she got married, Lucia kept to herself, but she paraded around the village to show off her new clothes, and she still had constant run-ins with her brother Alfonso. This had reinforced Mother's view that Lucia was both unreasonably headstrong – *caparbia* – and a tease – *a civetta* – to boot. These were two serious and dangerous faults in a new wife.

As the weather got colder, our minds had turned to the upcoming voyage, and Mother had set out to do what everyone else before her had done. She found a buyer for her wedding costume. Traditionally, the women were buried in their wedding clothes. During the war, many brides had borrowed one another's costumes, since the materials needed to make them were quite expensive. Now, as more and more women shed the traditional garb to go to America, they sold it for a few lire to those who remained without one of their own. No one thought of taking the traditional *pacchiana* clothes along as a souvenir; they were much too cumbersome to pack. She found room in the trunk for a black shawl and a lacy *mandile*.

Worrying about the trip had made my mother lose weight. When Giovanna took her measurements for two new dresses, Mother, deprived of the layers of clothing the costume had provided, hated herself in the mirror. "*Paru na sarda asciutta,*" she said in disgust, comparing herself to a dry herring. Despite trying on other colours, Mother chose blue for both dresses,

154

blue being the only colour she found neither too drab nor too showy. She insisted on the same style of modest round collar on both pieces. She also had to be measured for a bra, which, as a *pacchiana,* she had never worn. Because her breasts were almost non-existent, Giovanna stuffed the cups with leftover lining material, and then laughed at Mother screaming in protest because the two cups turned out too pointy.

I was also measured for a new dress — a pleated, brown woolen one with long sleeves — and a red wool coat. Lucia kept Giovanna working nights. She ordered dresses, skirts, a suit, and a coat with money sent by her new husband.

Mother started wearing the new dresses two weeks before leaving, just so she could get used to them. The next thing that needed attention was her hair. She had let her braids dangle to her shoulders, but my father had written that she should have her hair cut and permed. There were no hairdressers for women in Mulinera, so Zio had Don Cesare drive us to Catanzaro. Mother's hair was not as thick as most of the other women's. As long as she had kept it braided and puffed on the sides, this deficiency had not been too obvious, but as soon as the hairdresser cut it to a short chin-length, it just fell flat and separated at the crown, showing three bald patches, the results of carrying heavy loads on her head for years. "*Paru na gallina spinnata,*" she said.

From the expression on his face, the hairdresser seemed to agree that she looked like a plucked chicken. "Of course, you need a permanent," he said. Zio left us to attend to other business, while I sat and watched the whole procedure. The hairstylist rolled her hair on rods and then attached each rod to a clamp connected by a wire to a machine. I sat on the edge of my chair until the hairdresser finally disconnected mother from the dangerous-looking contraption. What if she needed to get up and run out of the store? When the permanent was finished, the hairdresser flattened the tightly-curled hair at the crown with some pomade, and then arranged it like a halo around her face and nape. Zio came back with a green cashmere hat and a small blue purse, both for me. As we walked back up from the piazza in the late afternoon, I felt like a new person, wearing my new hat and carrying my empty purse around my wrist. Mother looked very much like a city woman in her new dress and permed hair. She would never be able to make her hair look that good again. After a few days, it lost its halo shape. And when she tried washing it, it curled out of control. "*Mo, paru na crapa,*" she said, and said she wished she could pull it all off since it made her look like a goat.

As she packed the trunk and suitcases, Mother again wanted to pull her hair out, in exasperation this time. Besides our clothes and Mother's trousseau of bedspreads, embroidered sheets, and pillowcases, we had to find good hiding places for the heavy *capicolli, sopressata* and sausages. Everyone knew by now that cured meats were not allowed in the new country, yet everyone took chances. We felt that this was what our families were missing and valued most. The going joke was that, if the meat were confiscated, we should just eat it all in front of the customs agents. After all, there was no law against eating smoked salami before entering the country. The first bit of news that the villagers were anxious to hear was whether their salamis had made it through customs.

Mother could not refuse anyone. "If you refuse one then you have to refuse them all." We spent the last week stuffing the trunk and suitcases, and weighing them on the grocery store's scale since we were only allowed a specified maximum weight. The trunk was locked, tied, and sent in advance. The suitcases remained open until the day of our departure.

On the last Sunday, Mother took out the only piece of jewellery she owned, a gold chain given to her by her parents on her wedding day. She tied it around the neck of the statue of the Madonna del Rosario as an offering and a plea to help us through the long sea voyage.

On the morning we left, after I went to school for the last time to say goodbye to my classmates and to Signor Gavano, I passed the bar where everyone was waiting for the television to be delivered. I didn't stop because I had promised Mother I would go straight home and help repack the suitcases. The day was rainy and wet. As I walked up the hill, Aurora's mother,

Paola, came out of her house and waved at me to come inside. Her house smelled of cabbage and pork rind. She wiped her wet hands on her apron and planted a kiss on my face. "*Oh Catarinella, mia,*" she said. "So I won't be seeing you walk up anymore."

Then from her apron pocket, she pulled out a small *sopressata* wrapped in an oily paper, and insisted that I take it. "I'll come and see your mother later, but give her this to pack. If they take it, they take it. If it passes, then you'll eat it with my love when you get there." Then she kissed me again, and said, "*Va, va, bella mia, e buona fortuna.*"

I walked up, holding back the tears, holding on to the little gifts that my friends at school and Signor Gavano had given me. By late afternoon, my grandparents, uncles, aunts, and cousins started congregating at our house. Zio, swearing, had to get Luigi to stand on each suitcase so he could close them and tie them with a cord. By the evening, the house was packed with people, and the conversation centred on the TV show that they would soon be watching. When the time to leave got close, Nanna Stella started crying, and Zio got upset at her. "Stop the crying. They're going to America, not to a funeral."

When Don Cesare came with a couple of other men to get the suitcases, Zio started wailing like the others, embracing Luigi like he didn't want to let him go – even though Zio would be travelling with us to

Naples. From all that crying, I got the feeling that we were leaving Mulirena forever.

The train station at Santa Eufemia looked unfamiliar in the dark of night. I had taken a train there before, to go to Rome for our visas. It had been daylight, and the white-stucco station, with its rows of pink oleanders along one side and a palm tree on the other, had buzzed with the noises of trains and people jostling to get on and off.

The ten o'clock train for Naples was not there yet, but Don Cesare and Zio rushed to move the suitcases onto the platform as though we were late. Don Cesare shook hands with Mother, hugged my brother, and pinched me on the cheeks. Lucia stood back from us, not making any move to shake hands with him. As he walked away, he bent his head in her direction and said, "*Buona fortuna a tutti.*" Everyone became silent again.

It had rained here too, and the air was chilly. Mother hugged both Luigi and me to her body to keep us warm. After a few minutes, a family from Amato arrived by car and came to join us on the platform – a man and a young woman who was holding a sleeping child in her arms. I didn't know them, but Zio struck up a conversation with the man. He was the woman's brother and, like Zio, he was accompanying his sister to Naples. She would be taking the same boat as us, but then would remain on the train for another two days to go to Winnipeg to meet her husband, who had left just before her two-year-old son was born.

Zio said to the man, "You'll soon be going to Winnipeg too?"

"God willing," he answered.

The woman smiled and nodded at Zio, as she shifted her weight, rocking the heavy child, whose head rested on her shoulder. She didn't talk to anyone, but the woman had a constant smile on her face. She was so unlike Lucia, who neither cried nor smiled.

The sleeping child kept everyone quiet, but the silence was soon shattered by bells announcing the arrival of the Espresso train. It arrived so quickly and noisily, expelling steam on the rails, that Mother instinctively stepped back, hugging us closer to her. Zio, who took trains all the time, was the first to run toward it, dragging the two heaviest suitcases. We all followed him. He took the first empty cabin and arranged the suitcases on the shelves over the seats. The train, which was coming from Sicily, was not very full at that time of night, but judging from the amount of baggage in the corridors, most of the other passengers were headed for the same boat trip.

Zio found another empty cabin for himself and Luigi, so that we three ladies would have plenty of space to stretch out. We used our coats as pillows. Lucia and I lay on one seat, with our heads on opposite sides; my mother on the other.

Maybe feeling sorry for Lucia, who looked so forlorn, curled up on the bench in a fetal position, Mother said, "Departures are ugly for everyone."

I thought it especially ugly for Lucia who seemed snatched unnaturally from the love of her life, the only man she had ever loved, who ran away from her only because she reminded him of Mulirena. I curled up, too, on my side of the bench. I hardly slept, though. The whistling and the screeching of wheels as the train approached each station kept me awake. We had passed these cities twice before, and their names had become familiar – Benevento, Amantea, Salerno ...

On our other trips, we had passed rows and rows of tenement buildings built so close to the tracks that we could almost touch their balconies. I had noticed the peeling, stained stucco, the piled-up garbage. But the neighbourhoods had teemed with life. We saw women hanging clothes on these same balconies, the sheets and underwear flapping in the wind, while in the streets, small boys in sandals played soccer and waved at the train. I thought of the people sleeping in the dimly-lit apartments. They'd wake up in the morning to their normal routines. The children would go to school, the men to work and the women would go about their chores. They would know nothing of us, who had passed this way for the last time, sliding past them so quickly in the night.

Acknowledgements

The stories in this short novel originally formed part of a much longer work, a 600-page multilayered novel I presented as a Master's thesis at Concordia University in Montreal. Extracting them from their original context was painful but ultimately liberating. I would like to thank my publisher Linda Leith for taking a leap of faith that I would succeed in this, and for her firm guidance as an editor.

In the fourteen years since I started writing some of these stories, many people have helped me with critical feedback and moral support. It is to my first writing teachers at Concordia University that I owe the greatest gratitude. I'd like to single out Scott Lawrence, who made me believe that my stories were worth writing; Mary di Michele and Kate Sterns for their thorough reading of my thesis and valuable recommendations, and mostly Terry Byrnes, teacher extraordinaire, for his grace and patience as thesis supervisor and for guiding me through every phase of the writing. I'd also like to acknowledge the following people who have offered comments, suggestions, encouragement, and blunt criticism: Ann Diamond, Elettra Bedon, Antonio D'Alfonso, John Asfour, Julie Roorda, and Michael Mirolla. To my extended family, my close friends – you know who you are – my sons David and Anthony, and my daughter-in-law Melissa, thank you for being close to me at painful and happy times and for encouraging me in my passion for writing in spite of the sporadic state of amnesia it often caused.

This is a work of fiction. I was born in a Southern Italian village much like Mulirena. Real people, historical events and personal circumstances provided the initial inspiration for the stories that have shaped the work. Once on paper, however, my characters took on quirky and erratic lives of their own, refusing to obey common rules of discretion, so that any resemblance to actual people, living or dead has become entirely coincidental. That said, I would like to acknowledge the work of Antonio Caccetta, and his book, *Miglierina, un paese due campanili, il tempo e la memoria.* for the historical information used as background for the fictitious village of Mulirena. "Without historical memory," he wrote, "we lose our orientation and skip over our relationship with time, space, our own self and others."